Over 50 specially chosen stories and poems from the "People's Friend"
children's corner for boys and girls

Draw your special picture here. Remember, all good artists sign their work!

signed ....

stick photographs on this page,
or better still, draw
them yourself!

Grandma

To Ro............. OR ROSE

because you are so special. 4
Love and Hugs from

4 4 4
4

....

Date ....

Me

5

What's Inside

Poems with Activities

Short Stories

Tea Time
With A

HICKORY Dickory Dock," Sally recited. "The mouse ran up the clock." She loved the big grandfather clock at Granny and Grandad's house and she stood gazing up at it, waiting for it to chime.

Bong! Bong! Bong! Bong!

Sally clapped her hands as the sound died away. Then she thought about it.

"Why would a mouse want to run up the clock?" she said to herself.

A little head popped out from the top of the clock and looked down at her.

"Silly question!" the mouse said and peered at the time. "Ah, four o'clock. Tea time!"

He disappeared.

Sally stood gazing up in astonishment.

Suddenly the head popped back out again.

"Oh, I do beg your pardon! I was quite forgetting my manners. Would you like to come to tea?"

"Oh! Thank you. Y-y-yes, I would!" Sally stammered.

The head disappeared.

"Er, how do I get in?"

The head popped back out.

"Oh, I'm so sorry! Do please use the front door!"

There was indeed a door on the front of the clock with a

Difference

brass doorknob. Sally hesitated a moment then reached up and turned the knob. The door swung open.

"Do come in," the mouse called, "and please shut the door behind you."

Sally carefully stepped inside and obediently pulled the door to.

"Oh, and mind your head!"

Sally ducked just in time. The big brass pendulum swung over her head, backwards and forwards, backwards and forwards. Tick tock, tick tock.

THE clock was much bigger inside than she could have imagined and the mice had made it very homely. In front of her was a table laid with a smart, blue checked tablecloth.

Three little mice sat along one side of the table with napkins tied around their necks. They stared at Sally with big round eyes.

Mrs Mouse bustled about fetching an extra cup, saucer and plate from the dresser, and Mr Mouse pulled a chair up to the table.

"Do please sit down." Mrs Mouse smiled. "And help yourself!"

There were fish paste sandwiches and jam tarts and jelly and, of course, cheese. Mrs Mouse poured tea from a large brown teapot.

The little mice never took their eyes off Sally, but they said not one word. After tea was finished their mother looked at them.

"Right, time for bed! Don't forget to clean your teeth and wash behind your ears."

The little mice looked at Sally and whispered amongst themselves. Then they whispered to their mother, holding their little paws up in front of their mouths to shield what they were saying. Then they looked at Sally again

Mrs Mouse smiled and nodded. "I'll ask her." She turned to Sally.

"You're the first visitor we've ever had," she said. "And the children would like it so much if you could tell them a bedtime story."

"Of course!" Sally said and she followed the little mice into their bedroom. When she had finished the story she tucked them up in bed and kissed them goodnight.

Now it was time for her to go. Mr and Mrs Mouse stood up politely.

"Thank you so much for having me," Sally said, remembering her manners. "It was a very nice tea."

"Thank you," Mrs Mouse said, shaking her by the hand. "We're very glad you could come. And the children loved your story. Do come again!"

"Thank you, I'd like that!"

Mr Mouse saw her to the door.

"Mind your head!"

Sally carefully ducked her head as the pendulum swung backwards and forwards, backwards and forwards. Tick tock, tick tock.

As she stepped back out into the hallway Mr Mouse called after her.

"Now, don't forget — four o'clock! We always take tea at four o'clock!"

Sally closed the door behind her and stood for a moment looking up at the big grandfather clock.

Now she knew why the mouse ran up the clock!

9

Grannies
Are
Great!

10

GRANNIES are delightful things
For little girls and boys.
They never make a lot of fuss
When children make a noise.

They buy us comics, crisps and sweets
And other treats as well.
And if we're naughty now and then
Grannies never tell.

They're happy playing Dominoes
And Snakes-and-Ladders, too.
They always seem to let us win
For that's what Grannies do.

They let us have our favourite food
For breakfast, lunch and tea.
And never say a single thing
If we want to watch TV.

They read us bedtime stories
And tuck us in at night.
And never lose their temper
If we have a pillow fight.

Yes, Grannies are delightful things
It's very plain to see.
And if you have a Granny
I'm sure you will agree.

ACTIVITY

How great is your granny? Write a list of all the nice things your granny does for you!

Scraps' Surprise

IT was a snowy Christmas Eve. Scraps the scarecrow felt very chilly as he stood in the empty cornfield. Snowflakes were falling on to his ragged hat and the wind blew right through his old patched coat.

"Hello, Scraps!" his friend Ruby Robin called out.

Ruby flew down to perch on Scraps' tattered hat.

"Are you looking forward to Christmas Day tomorrow?" she chirped excitedly.

Scraps shook his head.

"I'm not bothering about Christmas this year." He shivered. "I don't expect Santa will bring me a present anyway!"

Ruby was shocked to hear this. So was William Wren who had been listening.

"Haven't you sent Santa a letter?" William asked. "We always write to him early each winter."

Scraps hadn't even thought about writing to Santa. He felt very cold and sad indeed.

"Poor Scraps. He really needs cheering up." Ruby sighed.

"And warming up, too!" William agreed. "We must do something."

The two friends finally decided that they would write a letter to Santa for Scraps.

"I hope there's still time for the letter to reach Santa," William said anxiously.

"Yes, Santa likes to get his presents sorted out early," Ruby replied. "He may not have one left for poor Scraps!"

THERE was no time to lose! Ruby looked out her pad and pen and wrote out the letter straight away.

Dear Santa,
Our friend Scraps the scarecrow gets very cold standing in the field all day. Please send him a special Christmas present to cheer him up!
Love from Ruby and William.
P.S. We hope this note isn't too late!

Ruby and William were very pleased with their letter and hurried to post it. But when they reached the post-box they had a terrible shock. A big sign was stuck across the front which read NO POST UNTIL AFTER CHRISTMAS!

"What a disappointment!" Ruby cried.

"Scraps will never get his present now!" William frowned. "We've left it too late!"

But Ruby had an idea.

"I'll pop the note in my Christmas stocking tonight." She laughed. "Santa's sure to see it when he delivers my presents!"

"You are clever, Ruby!" William giggled. "I just hope Santa has brought a spare gift with him on his sleigh."

The two little birds said goodbye and promised to meet in Scraps' field in the morning. And the very last thing Ruby did before going to bed was to put Scraps' note in her stocking.

ON Christmas morning Ruby woke up bursting with excitement.

Her stocking was bulging with goodies and she also noticed immediately that her letter had gone!

Quickly the little robin hurried out to meet William in Scraps' field. William was already there and both he and Scraps looked terribly excited.

"Look! Santa has left me a present!" Scraps gasped. "I wanted to wait until you were both here before I opened it."

There was also a note attached to the parcel. Scraps asked Ruby to read it out.

Dear Scraps,
Mrs Santa packed me this spare (in case I got the one I was wearing wet with snow!) I do hope you like it.
Love from Santa. X

Of course Scraps couldn't wait to unwrap his present. It was a wonderful, new bright red coat, just like the one Santa always wore!

Ruby and William helped Scraps put it on. It was so cosy and warm, and it fitted perfectly.

"You won't feel the cold wearing that!" Ruby chirped.

"And you look very smart," William added, smiling.

Scraps was so happy.

"This is wonderful!" he cried. "My best Christmas present ever! But I wonder how Santa found out about me?"

Ruby and William looked at each other and smiled secretly.

"I guess a little bird told him!" Ruby joked. And they all laughed.

13

14

Tom The Town Crier

TOM CROW was a fine bird, everybody said so. He had such lovely, shiny black feathers and keen, beady eyes. He was always so friendly, too, and did his best to help everyone. But the trouble was Tom made such a noise.

He couldn't help it. It was the way he was made. He tried not to let it get him down, but sometimes he had to sigh a great sigh when he heard his friends Nicky Nightingale and Thora Thrush singing so sweetly, or when he heard Clive the Cuckoo sing out his cheerful "Cuck-coo! Cuck-coo!" or even when he heard the chaffinches chattering away.

Tom kept hoping that one day he would be able to sing sweetly himself, or at least make a noise that didn't have the other birds clapping their wings over their ears. But it was no good. Every time he opened his beak, all that came out was "CAW! CAW! CAW!"

His friends tried not to complain because they were very fond of Tom. But sometimes they couldn't help themselves.

"Tom," Nicky Nightingale said one day, "I know you're a very fine crow, a very fine crow indeed! But please can you keep your beak shut sometimes?"

Well, Tom didn't think that was at all fair as he kept his beak shut far more than the other birds and went for hours without saying a thing. It was just that when he did say something, everybody noticed it.

Some days poor Tom was so miserable he kept quiet nearly all day. He didn't even want to hear his own voice.

ONE day, Mr Magpie the mayor came strutting along, looking very smart and splendid with his robes and chain.

"There's going to be a contest to find the best town crier!" he announced. "And I think we can win it!"

"I'm sure we can," Nicky Nightingale said. "But, please, Mr Mayor, what's a town crier?"

Mr Magpie smiled.

"It's someone who wears splendid robes - almost as splendid as mine! They ring a bell and cry 'OYEZ, OYEZ,' to tell everyone what's going on!"

"That sounds easy," Nicky Nightingale said.

But though her voice was sweet it wasn't very loud.

"That's a lovely noise," Mr Magpie said. "But you need to be heard far and wide!"

Thora Thrush and Clive Cuckoo tried, too, and so did the chattering chaffinches, but their voices were all too quiet.

"No, I'm sorry." Mr Magpie shook his head. "It's not a contest for sweet singing."

Now, Tom Crow had been listening in and wondered if he dared . . . Was this something he might be good at?

"Please, Mr Mayor, let me try," he said.

"By all means," the mayor said as he was very fond of Tom Crow.

Well, when Tom opened his beak, everyone knew that they'd found their town crier. He made such a wonderfully loud noise!

I think you know what happened next. Tom was kitted out with robes nearly as splendid as Mr Magpie's and given a bell to ring, and he strutted around practising to his heart's content.

"CAW-YEZ! CAW-YEZ!"

And Tom was voted the best and loudest town crier that anyone had ever known.

All his friends are so proud of him and some of them say he's going to be the next mayor. But Tom doesn't want to be. Oh, no, he's much happier being the town crier!

JEREMY THE GIANT

LONG ago, in a faraway land, there lived a giant called Jeremy. He towered above all the people who lived there and he was taller than the tallest trees in the forest.

But Jeremy wasn't a happy giant. He didn't like being so much taller than everyone else, especially as all the children thought he looked quite scary.

Sometimes he would look

down and watch them chatting and laughing together. He wished so much that he could join in. But each time he opened his mouth to say something, the words came bellowing out so loudly that they frightened everyone. The people would run inside their homes and bolt their doors.

No wonder Jeremy felt so lonely!

Deep down, Jeremy was kind and loving, a real gentle giant.

ONE day, Jeremy caught the worst cold he'd ever had. He kept sneezing so loudly that he blew the leaves off the trees. In fact, his "A-aa-TISH-oos" could be heard from one end of the land to the other. The earth even began to shake, making some people wonder if they were having a tremendous earthquake!

Jeremy wished he could stop sneezing. He hated frightening everyone.

After a few days Jeremy finally stopped sneezing. His throat still felt rather sore, though.

"I hope I feel better soon." He sighed. "It's not nice having a told in my doze."

It was then he realised that he'd lost his voice — well, almost. Instead of bellowing out his words as usual, he was now only able to whisper.

And Jeremy's whisper sounded just like everyone else's normal voice!

"I love my new voice." Jeremy smiled. "Nobody will feel afraid of me now when I speak."

He felt so happy with his soothing, soft voice that he began singing a lullaby.

Soon everyone in the land stopped what they were doing and began listening to Jeremy singing.

"Maybe we've all been wrong about Jeremy," someone said. "Any giant who can sing so sweetly must be a gentle giant and not scary at all."

"It's not his fault he's so tall, either, and he has no friends," everyone agreed. "He must get very lonely.

They were now beginning to feel very sorry for Jeremy.

"Let's ask him to join us so we can get to know him better," they suggested.

"Come over here with us, Jeremy," they called

out. "We promise we won't run away."

Jeremy could hardly believe what they said. He walked slowly towards them, taking care not to stamp his great big feet as he walked. He knew he had to show them that he was a gentle giant!

AS time went by, Jeremy made lots of friends. Everyone liked him. Sometimes he found he was glad to be so tall, especially when he was able to retrieve balls and cats from the tops of trees, making tearful children smile again.

Nowadays, Jeremy doesn't have time to feel lonely. He's too busy helping all his new friends. You see, when high buildings need painting, or someone's roof needs repairing, they always ask Jeremy to do those jobs for them. After all, Jeremy doesn't need a ladder!

Best of all, though, Jeremy is now a happy giant, and anyone who knows him thinks that he is the best biggest friend anyone could have.

17

Hamish Has A Problem

YOUNG HAMISH the hedgehog woke up one day at the time of red and gold leaves. He felt different from usual. He sniffed the air.

"Brr, it's cold," he said to himself.

"Of course it is," said a robin nearby. "Winter's coming. You'd better get ready."

"Get ready? How do I get ready?" asked Hamish, but the robin had flown away.

I'd better go and ask some of my friends at the farm how they're getting ready for winter, thought Hamish, and off he went to the farm.

The first friend he met was Bessie the red and white cow.

"Hello, Bessie. Winter's coming. How are you getting ready for it?"

"I'll be all right," said Bessie. "Mr Jones, the farmer, is taking me into the warm cowshed today and he'll give me turnips and hay to eat. It'll be lovely. I'm looking forward to it."

Just then Mr Jones came for Bessie.

"Bye till spring, Hamish," said Bessie.

"Bye, Bessie," said Hamish.

Snowball the white horse was galloping round his field.

"D'you know that winter's coming, Snowball?" asked Hamish. "Are you getting ready?"

"Yes, Hamish," said Snowball. "Mr Jones has bought me a warm blanket to wear outside when it's cold and he's put straw on the stable floor to keep my hooves warm. Everything's ready for the cold winter days. You'd better get ready, too."

"What should I do?" asked Hamish, but Snowball was off galloping again and didn't hear him.

Beneath a tree were some squirrels digging in the earth with their paws.

"What are you doing?" Hamish asked.

"Burying some nuts to eat in the winter," said the squirrels. "Have you hidden your nuts? You'd better get ready."

"I don't eat nuts," said Hamish. "What should I be doing to get ready for winter?"

"Hide some nuts, hide some nuts," said the squirrels climbing up the tree to their dreys as fast as they could.

Hamish reached the farm yard. Fluff the cat was there.

"Are you ready for winter, Fluff?" asked Hamish.

"In winter I stay indoors most of the time. There'll be cushions and cream and warm fires. Very nice – winter."

HAMISH was just going to ask Fluff what he should do when Rover the dog came bounding along.

"Hello, Hamish. I must tell the children you're here. They always like to see you," and he ran to the farmhouse door and barked.

Sam and Sally dashed out, wondering what all the noise was about.

"It's our favourite hedgehog," cried Sally.

"I'll fetch his cat food and water," said Sam.

When Hamish had eaten the cat food and taken a long drink of water, the children sat down beside him and stroked his furry nose.

"Soon you'll not come to see us, little hedgehog," said Sam.

"Yes, you'll curl up into a spiky ball, and go to sleep for the winter," said Sally.

So that's what I must do to get ready for the winter, thought Hamish. Sally had solved his problem. He was happy that at last he knew what to do. I'll go home to my hedge and get curled up at once, he decided. And off he went,

"Bye till spring," called the children.

19

The Frog

FRED the Frog seemed very fond
Of sitting on the lily pond.
Quite content to simply stay
Basking in the sun all day.

His friends quite often sighed and said,
"Won't you come and join us, Fred?
Don't you want to come and play,
Not just sit on that pond all day?"

But Fred just sat there, loudly croaking,
"My friends, I think you must be joking!
I'm quite content to watch you play
And sit here on the pond all day."
He watched them playing bat and ball
And didn't fancy that at all.
Of football he just wasn't fond —
He much preferred his lily pond!

His friends all thought it such a shame,
They often stopped and called his name.
"Oh, please, Fred, won't you come and play,
Not just sit on the pond all day?"

But Fred just sat there, green and squat,
And croaked his answer, "I will NOT!"
So there was nothing to be done —
They went past him, one by one.

And Fred sat there and watched them play,
On his lily pond all day,
and thought, I'd be no good at all
At playing catch or bat and ball!

One day he heard a stirring sound —
"Look! What's that? What's this we've found?
Can it really be? . . . Let's hope
That we have found a skipping rope!"

It was indeed and so that day
They had a brand new game to play.
But none of them was good at skipping!
The rope got tangled, they kept tripping!

Fred watched and wondered, could it be
That this is the right game for me?
And he let out a croaking cry,
"My friends, please let me have a try!"

Well, you just had to stop and stare
To see Fred bouncing in the air
And shouting out, with croaks of glee,
"Yes, skipping IS the game for me!"

21

April Showers

ONE morning in the month of April, Eileen went to spend the day with her grandma and grandpa.

"What do you want to do today, Eileen?" Grandma asked.

"I'd like to help you," Eileen said.

"All right," Grandma said. "You can help me bake some little cakes for our elevenses. Would you like to do that?"

"Oh, yes," Eileen cried and she ran to get the blue apron that Grandma had made for her to wear when she was helping at Grandma and Grandpa's house.

Eileen helped to measure all the things to make little cakes. Grandma let her take turns at mixing and beating the mixture with a wooden spoon, and then putting spoonfuls of the creamy mixture into paper cake cases.

Then Grandma popped a tray of cakes into the oven and they washed up the bowls and spoons they'd used.

Grandma was just taking out the cakes, which were now golden brown, when Grandpa came in.

"Those cakes smell good," Grandpa said. "Can I have some?"

"We'll have them for our elevenses," Grandma said.

"Great!" Grandpa said.

"Could we have our elevenses in the garden among the daffodils?" Eileen asked.

"What a good idea," Grandma said. "Could you and Grandpa set out the picnic tables and chairs?"

When the table and chairs were out on the grassy lawn, Grandma and Eileen spread a pretty cloth over the table and set out three plates, three mugs, a milk jug and sugar bowl, and a plate with the cakes on it.

"Let's put some daffodils in the middle of the table," Grandma suggested. "You can pick some, Eileen, while I go indoors for a vase."

"I'm coming indoors for some things, too," Grandpa said.

"What are you going for, Grandpa?" Eileen asked.

"You'll see in a little while," Grandpa said. "If I can find them."

As Eileen picked the daffodils she wondered what Grandpa would bring out.

A little while later he came into the garden carrying three umbrellas.

"Grandpa, why have you brought umbrellas?" Eileen cried.

"I'm wondering the same," Grandma said, putting the daffodils into a glass vase. "The sun's not hot enough for sun shades and it's not raining, so we don't need umbrellas."

"Wait and see," Grandpa said laying the umbrellas down.

Grandma brought out the coffee pot. Grandpa brought a jug of orange juice for Eileen and they all sat down to have their elevenses.

SUDDENLY, the sun stopped shining. Eileen looked up at the sky. Clouds were covering the sun. Then she noticed something.

"Look!" she cried. "There's a rainbow."

Quickly, Grandpa picked up and opened the umbrellas, giving Grandma and Eileen one each.

"It'll just be a shower," he said. "It'll soon pass."

"What a good idea to bring the umbrellas," Grandma said as the raindrops pitter-pattered down.

"Did you see the rain clouds coming, Grandpa? Was that why you brought the umbrellas?" Eileen asked.

"Yes, Eileen," Grandpa said. "But I remembered, too, that it's April and in April we get showers."

"Yes," Grandma said. "We should be glad when they come for April showers bring May flowers."

"That's a nice little poem," Eileen said. "I'll try to remember it always."

23

The Magic Pool

MARCY and Kevin had just moved into a new home. The best thing so far was the huge garden. It was perfect for races, all kinds of games and trees for playing hide-and-seek. They were exploring while the moving men took furniture and boxes into the house and their parents were very busy.

"Look! Come here, Marcy," Kevin called from a corner of the garden where there was a gate with bars.

Marcy ran over to Kevin who was standing at the edge of the garden, peering through the fence at a big stone horse trough.

"What is it?" Marcy asked. "It looks like a magic pool. Let's make a wish," she said. "What should it be?"

"A pony!" Kevin said quickly. "That would be perfect in this garden."

Peering down into the dark water, they said together, "We wish, we wish, we wish — for a pony."

They waited, but nothing happened.

Then they both squealed. In the water they saw the shape of a pony's head!

"It's true, our wish has come true!" Marcy said, her eyes wide.

"I can't believe it." Kevin stepped back from the fence. "Move back here a bit. It might jump out."

They waited. They kept looking, but the pony's head had vanished.

"Oh, it's gone! It wasn't magic after all," Marcy said sadly.

Something was nudging Kevin's shoulder from behind and he looked around quickly.

"Marcy, look! It's the pony!" They jumped up.

"It's REAL!"

THE children touched the pony's brown face and stroked its long mane.

When they ran to the house to tell their mum and dad, the pony trotted behind them. Their parents, still busy unpacking boxes, were very surprised, too.

"Where could it have come from?"

The children said it had come from their wish in the magic pool.

A man was running across the grass and they heard him shouting.

"So there you are, Jerry! What are you doing here?" He came up to the family.

"Hello! I'm your neighbour, John Sims," he said, out of breath. "Jerry wandered away through my hedge, but I knew I'd probably find him here."

"Didn't he come out of the pool?" Marcy asked.

Mr Sims looked puzzled.

"We made a wish and saw the pony in the water," Kevin added, "but then it was behind us on the grass."

Mr Sims laughed.

"That was his reflection you saw in the trough. But Jerry's real, not magic. He is used to coming over here. The family that has just moved away had three children and he loved giving them rides."

Marcy tugged at her father's sleeve.

"Can he still come over, please? We'd have fun and Jerry would, too. Please, Dad, Mum, Mr Sims?"

The three grown-ups talked together for a minute, then they said that would be fine. Everybody shook hands and the children thanked their new neighbour.

"So the pool was magic after all!" Kevin said.

"Well — in a way." Mr Sims smiled.

Jerry the pony snorted and they looked around. He was nodding his head as if he was saying, "Yes! YES!"

Mother's Day Surprise

CLAIRE was so worried. Soon it would be Mother's Day and she wanted to give her mother a nice gift, but being only six years old she didn't have much money. She only had eighty pence in her piggy bank!

What can I get for eighty pence, she wondered? She could think of nothing worth buying for Mummy which cost so little. Then she had a good idea. She would talk to Grandma. Grandma was sure to come up with some useful suggestions.

A few days later Grandma called for morning coffee. While Mummy was busy in the kitchen Claire asked her grandma for advice.

"What can I give Mummy for Mother's Day which only costs eighty pence?"

Grandma thought for a moment.

"I have an idea," she said.

"When your mummy was a little girl she was very fond of wild flowers. She loved buttercups, daisies, bluebells, cowslips and so on. She used to say she would love a garden full of wild flowers.

"Now you could give one to her! If you buy her a packet of wild flower seeds, she could make a wild flower garden in that spare patch of ground at the bottom of the garden."

"I like that," Claire said. "But why are they called wild flowers, Grandma? That's a funny name."

"They are flowers which live in this country naturally and grow in the wild," her Grandma told her.

That afternoon Claire and her grandma went shopping at the garden centre. Claire soon found the display of seeds. She was pleased to see that a packet of wild flower seeds only cost seventy pence, so she had plenty of money to buy them!

Back home again, Claire hid the packet of seeds away until Mother's Day. Her brother and sister wondered what she was going to give their mummy.

"You'll have to wait to find out," she told them.

On Mother's Day, Claire's sister gave Mummy a bottle of perfume and her brother gave her a box of chocolates.

"I wonder what this can be?" Mummy said as she opened Claire's surprise parcel. She was delighted to see the packet of wild flower seeds.

"How lovely!" she exclaimed. "I have always wanted a wild flower garden. How did you guess, Claire? You are clever!"

LATER that day Daddy dug over the little patch of ground in the garden and all the children helped to rake it until it was smooth and free of lumps. Then they watched as Mummy sprinkled the seeds over the ground.

"I can't wait to see my new wild garden," Mummy said. "Now, who is going to help me to eat these lovely chocolates?"

Donald's

DONALD the donkey was extremely disappointed. It was his birthday and none of the other donkeys in the field had wished him a happy birthday. He felt so dejected that he decided to go for a walk round the field and not bother to have any breakfast.

He noticed that the gate leading into the field had not been padlocked, so he decided to slip out while all the other donkeys were eating their breakfast. Very quietly, he closed the gate behind him and began to walk down the lane towards the village.

Donald hadn't gone far when he saw Mr Smith digging in his garden.

"Hello, Donald," Mr Smith said. "I've dug up some carrots for my dinner. Would you like one?"

"Yes, please. I do feel rather hungry," Donald replied.

Mr Smith washed one of the carrots in the rain-water barrel and gave it to Donald. It was delicious!

"Thank you, Mr Smith," Donald said. "Do you

Walkabout

know that's the nicest carrot I've ever tasted!"

And he continued his walk down the lane.

He had only gone a little way when he met Mrs Brown, who was carrying a large basket full of apples.

"Hello, Donald," she said. "Would you like an apple?"

"Yes, please, Mrs Brown," Donald said. "I am a bit hungry."

Mrs Brown picked out the nicest, biggest, rosiest, apple in the basket and gave it to Donald. It was lovely and Donald said it was the best apple he had ever tasted. He thanked his kind friend and continued his journey down the lane.

As he was passing the baker's shop he saw Betty, the farmer's daughter, coming out of the shop with a bag of buns.

"Hello, Donald," Betty said. "I've been buying buns for tea and the baker gave me one extra. He said it was because he had given me a baker's dozen. Would you like one?"

"Yes, please," Donald said. "I am quite hungry."

Betty picked out a nice, sticky, fruity bun and gave it to Donald.

The bun tasted wonderful.

"Thank you, Betty," Donald said. "That was the nicest bun I've ever had." And off he went down the lane.

At the bottom of the lane Donald saw two of his old friends, Hetty and Harry. They were hikers and they were sitting on the stile eating sandwiches.

"We were just coming to see you, Donald," Hetty said. "We thought you might like a sandwich."

"That would be lovely," Donald said. "I think I could just manage a sandwich."

"You can have a salad sandwich or a jam sandwich," Harry said. "Or would you like both?"

"Just one will do," Donald replied. "I don't feel very hungry, but I do love jam sandwiches."

The sandwich was delicious and Donald began to feel quite full up. He decided to go back to the field and have a snooze.

AFTER thanking Hetty and Harry he retraced his steps and wandered towards home. Luckily, the gate was still unpadlocked, so he was able to creep in. But his friends had been watching out for him.

"Where have you been?" they asked. "The farmer's wife has been looking for you."

"I went for a walk. Why does she want me?" Donald replied.

"To give you this," one of the donkeys said. "It's your birthday cake, of course. Happy birthday, Donald. We hadn't forgotten — we were waiting for the cake."

Donald was so pleased that he nearly burst with happiness.

"How wonderful," he said. "I'll cut it into six slices and we'll all have a piece."

Very carefully, Donald cut the cake into six pieces — five nice big ones for his friends and a smaller one for himself.

After all, he wasn't really hungry!

29

SNOWMAN

IT was snowing and snowing, and snowing again.
"Let's play in the garden," said Katy to Ben.
So they put on their hats and their scarves
and their coats,
And they put on their gloves and their wellington boots.

There was snow on the fence,
There was snow on the trees
And the snow on the ground
Came right up to their knees!

Ben made a snowball and threw it at Kate.
Kate threw it back and it stuck on the gate.
Soon snowballs were flying high up in the air.
It was cold, wet and chilly - but they didn't care!

"Let's make a snowman," Ben said to Kate.
"We'd better start now, before it gets late."
So they piled up the snow till it grew big and tall,
And they made it a head with a giant snowball.

"It's as big as our daddy, as big as can be!
Let's find it some glasses now so it can see!
And a hat and a scarf to keep out the cold,
And some woolly grey whiskers to make him look old!"

They started to run to the doorway, but then
Something squashy and wet came and landed on Ben!
"Hi!" Ben said. "Who did that? It's all very queer -
A snowball just hit me and nobody's near!"

Ben looked all round and Kate looked all round
But nobody! NOBODY else could be found!
Only the snowman, all gleaming white -
It gave the children quite a fright!

The snowman laughed. "It's quite OK,
I only want to join the play.
I only want to have some fun,
Let's throw some snow at everyone!"

He threw some snow at Ben and Kate,

And then he slid towards the gate
And started throwing snow again
At people who were in the lane.

The postman, who was on his way
To post some letters, joined the play,
And threw some snow at Kate and Ben,
So they both threw some back again!

The snowman cried, "I think it's great
To do this while it's not too late.
It's great for me to have some fun
Before I'm melted by the sun!"

And so they all of them set to,
Till Kate and Ben were wet right through!
At last they had to go inside
And get themselves cleaned up and dried.

Next day the sun was bright and hot,
But of the snowman there was not
The smallest trace, although the pair
Went searching,
  searching everywhere!

ACTIVITY

How many seagulls
can you see?

. . . .

Valentines

you don't write your name on it, you just write From your Valentine," Rachel replied. "Who are you giving yours to, Mark?"

"Mum, of course."

"Well, I'm going to make one for Dad."

"I'd like to make one, too," Joanna said. "But who will I give it to?"

"Yes, who will you give a Valentine to, Joanna?" Rachel wondered. "Mum and Dad are each getting one, and there's nobody else in our house."

The children got a card each out of the drawing box.

"What are you going to draw on yours, Rachel?" Mark asked.

"A car, decorated with pink ribbons and hearts," Rachel answered. "Dad is very fond of cars."

"Mum likes cars, too," Mark said, "but I should draw something different for her. What do you think it should be, Rachel?"

IT'S going to be Valentine's Day next week," Rachel told her brother, Mark, and little sister, Joanna.

"I know," Mark said. "My teacher told us. I'm going to make a Valentine card!"

"What's a Valentine card?" Joanna asked.

"It's a card for somebody you love. But

"Well, Mum is very fond of chocolates and flowers, and she likes pretty clothes and bangles and things."

"Then I will draw her all dressed up among the flowers in the garden," Mark decided.

"Don't forget to draw hearts. Valentine cards always have them," Rachel reminded him.

"I don't know what to draw on my Valentine," Joanna said sadly.

JUST then Mummy called the children into the kitchen.

"We have to go to the shops," she told them. "Please put on your coats."

"May I whisper something to you, Mummy?" Joanna asked.

"Yes, of course. What do you want to tell me?"

So Joanna whispered to Mummy that she didn't know what to draw on her Valentine card, and that she didn't know who to give it to.

"Don't worry," Mummy whispered back. "We'll look at all the Valentine cards in the newspaper shop. Then you'll get lots of ideas for making one, and I'm sure you will think of somebody to give it to."

After they had done their shopping they looked at all the Valentine cards which were decorated with hearts, ribbons, bows and flowers, and all sorts of pretty things.

On the way back home they met Miss Harvey, the old lady who lived next door. She was carrying two bags of shopping.

"Let us carry your bags," Mummy said.

So Rachel and Mark each took one of Miss Harvey's bags.

"I'll hold your hand, Miss Harvey," Joanna offered.

"That is kind of you all," Miss Harvey said, taking Joanna's hand.

When they reached Miss Harvey's gate, her big, black cat, Peter, was waiting for her.

The children stroked him and said how lovely he was.

"Yes, he is," Miss Harvey agreed, "and I do love him."

"I know what I'm going to draw on my Valentine's card," Joanna told Mummy when they went into their house. "A big, black cat like Peter — and I'll put it through Miss Harvey's letter-box on Valentine's Day!"

WHEN Valentine's Day came, Mummy invited Miss Harvey round for a cup of tea and a heart-shaped cake.

"What a lovely surprise I had today," Miss Harvey told them. "I got a Valentine card — the nicest one ever. And it had a picture of Peter on it! I wonder who my Valentine is? Whoever it is has made me very happy."

"That's nice," Mummy said and Joanna smiled her happiest smile.

33

The Very Busy Easter Bunny

DEEP in his secret underground burrow, Bobtail, the Easter Bunny, was hard at work. It was very nearly Easter Day and he had so much to do!

"Mmmm, yummy!" Bobtail smiled as he tasted the chocolate mixture he was making for his Easter eggs. "All the girls and boys will love eating my Easter eggs this year!"

Suddenly, while Bobtail was adding a few more special ingredients to the melted chocolate, he heard a worried voice.

"Help! Help! Is anyone there?" Bobtail wiped his

sticky paws on his already chocolate-covered apron and hurried outside to see what was the matter. He soon found a very tearful Molly Mouse.

"Oh! Bobtail!" Molly cried. "I was playing with my brand-new kite when a sudden gust of wind blew it right to the top of the oak tree! I'm too scared to climb up. Could you help, please?"

Bobtail wasn't very good at climbing trees either, but he didn't like to see Molly so upset. So, very carefully, he inched higher and higher up the branches.

"Got it!" Bobtail cried.

Molly smiled gratefully.

"Would you like to play with me?"

"I can't!" Bobtail said. "I must finish making my Easter eggs!" And he hurried back.

Inside his burrow, Bobtail poured his chocolate mixture into special egg moulds. When they had set hard he began to decorate and wrap each egg.

But, moments later, Bobtail heard another cry for help!

"I'm lost! I can't find my way home!"

Bobtail hopped outside to find little Basil Badger wandering about.

"Don't worry, Basil!" Bobtail said, taking his paw. "I know where you live. I'll take you home right now!"

Basil was relieved when he saw his mummy again.

"Oh, Basil!" she cried, hugging him. "Didn't I tell you not to run off?" Then Mrs Badger invited Bobtail in for tea.

But Bobtail had to get back!

"It's Easter Day tomorrow and I've not finished wrapping my Easter eggs yet!" he said. "I have to get up at dawn, too, to hide the eggs in the fields for the children to find!"

BOBTAIL rushed home, but he was running late. By midnight he still had more eggs to stack into baskets.

It was after daybreak when he set off to hide the eggs.

"Oh, if only I had someone to help me!" He sighed. "The children might not get their eggs this year!"

Suddenly — and Bobtail

didn't understand how this happened — Molly and Basil and their families appeared!

"We know how busy you've been, but you stopped to help us!" Molly told Bobtail. "Now we're all here to help you hide the Easter eggs so the children aren't disappointed!"

"Oh, thank you!" Bobtail cried happily. He handed everyone a basket brimming with shiny, wrapped Easter eggs. "Come on! There's no time to lose!"

So all the animals set off excitedly across the fields. They hid the eggs behind bushes, inside tree hollows and anywhere they could think of. It was great!

They finished just in time and went back to Bobtail's secret burrow for some chocolate tasting as well!

So, if you happened to be up very early on Easter morning, you might have seen some very funny goings-on in the fields. Perhaps it was Bobtail and his friends. You never know!

35

THE SNIFFLY-SNUFFLY PIG

ONCE there was a little pig called Pinky. He lived on a farm with Mother and Father Pig and his six brothers and three sisters. One day, Pinky and his six brothers and three sisters went out into the meadow to play.

They chased the yellow butterflies. They dug for sweet, tasty roots and rolled in the long grass. Then the little pigs lay down under a shady tree to rest — all except Pinky.

Pinky didn't want to rest. He wanted to play. There were so many things for a little pig to see and do. There were so many things to explore with his sniffly-snuffly nose.

Pinky raced away across the meadow looking for fun.

A snail was crawling slowly across the grass. What a funny-looking creature it was, with its shell on its back and its eyes on the end of stalks.

"Hello, snail," Pinky said, sniffing and poking the snail with his sniffly-snuffly nose. "Do you want to play?"

Then, the most amazing thing happened. The snail's eyes shrank back into its head and the head disappeared into the shell.

Pinky waited for the snail to come out again. He waited and waited, but the snail didn't want to play, so Pinky hurried on.

Soon Pinky saw a tiny ant scurrying along. The little pig followed with his sniffly-snuffly nose close to the ground.

"Hello, ant," Pinky said. "Do you want to play?"

But the ant didn't want to play. It came to its nest and disappeared into a hole in the ground. Pinky sat down near the hole to wait. He waited and waited, but the ant wouldn't come out to play, so Pinky hurried on.

Down by the duck pond, the little pig came upon a fat, green frog.

"Oh, good," Pinky said. "Here's a fat, green frog. He will play with me."

Pinky padded down to the water's edge. Sniff!

Sniff! He poked the frog with his sniffly-snuffly nose.

"Croak!" said the fat, green frog and jumped into the water.

"Oh, dear! Isn't there anyone who will play with me?" Pinky said to himself.

Suddenly there was a rustling, scratching sound coming from the reeds. Pinky pricked up his ears. He sniffed the air with his sniffly-snuffly nose.

A hedgehog came out of the reeds. It looked like a scrubbing brush with little feet and a pointy snout.

"Oh, goody!" Pinky said. "Hello, hedgehog, would you like to play with me?" Pinky gave the hedgehog a gentle poke with his sniffly-snuffly nose.

"Ouch!" Pinky squealed and the hedgehog gave an angry grunt and curled itself into a prickly ball. Pinky ran away as quickly as he could. When he came to the farmer's orchard, he sat down to rest.

"Buzz . . . buzz . . . buzz!" A fat bumblebee landed on a blossom near Pinky's head. Pinky watched the bee as it gathered nectar with its tongue.

"Hello, bee," Pinky said, but the bumblebee flew off before Pinky could ask him if he wanted to play.

POOR PINKY! He sat down among the buttercups feeling so sad and lonely. No-one wanted to be his friend. No-one wanted to play with him.

"Hello, little pig."

Pinky jumped in surprise. A little brown rabbit with long ears and a wiggly-twitchy nose was looking at him.

"Hello," the rabbit said again. "My name is Bunnykins and I'm looking for someone to play with me."

Well, I'm sure you can guess what happened. A sniffly-snuffly nose kissed a wiggly-twitchy nose.

"I'll play with you, Bunnykins," Pinky shouted happily and the little pink pig and the little brown rabbit ran off together to play in the meadow. **37**

JACK was feeling happy. Mum told him she was going to take him into town to buy a pair of trainers. He wanted some just like his big brother had but Mum said he must wait until he was older and then she would think about it. But if he kept on and on he wouldn't have any at all.

So Jack kept quiet as a mouse for ages. Now it was Saturday and he was off to buy the trainers. It was a long bus ride to town and when they got off in the middle of the High Street he hopped from foot to foot hoping they would go to the little shoe shop on the corner first.

But Mum wanted to go to the supermarket before it got too crowded. She said he had to be patient. Jack thought that was a really funny word

Jack's New Trainers

because it reminded him of going to the dentist when the nice girl there called out next patient please!

While he was thinking about this Mum filled her basket with fruit and other things, and then they had to stand in the check-out queue for ages.

Jack kept looking down at his feet wishing they could hurry and got to the little shoe shops.

And then, they did!

All the shelves were piled high with shoes and sandals and then, right at the very top of the shop, there were a whole lot of trainers. Lots and lots of different colours. Mum said he could choose.

Jack knew exactly the pair he wanted. They were white with a blue and a red stripe all the way round and nice thick laces that looked easy to tie. Mum liked them, too, and smiled at another lady whose little boy was also choosing trainers.

Only he couldn't make up his mind. This boy's mother told him to hurry up, she hadn't got all day. So then he made up his mind quickly.

Mum and the other lady went to the counter to pay the money.

The girl put the trainers in a big cardboard box and Jack hugged it to his chest. When they came out onto the pavement they found it was pouring with rain and they hurried to the bus stop. They'd just missed one so had to wait ages.

As soon as they got home Jack carefully undid the box and took all the tissue paper out. There were the trainers, looking lovely and bright and new. Mum laughed and said they wouldn't look like that in a few days!

Jack pushed his feet into them but his heels just wouldn't go in even though Mum helped.

"I can't understand it," Mum said. "Surely the rain couldn't have shrunk them?" Then Mum turned them over. "Oh!" she cried. "Look, Jack. They're the wrong size! They are too small for your feet."

Jack nearly burst into tears. He had to swallow hard. Mum put her arms round him.

"I know what has happened," she said. "The girl mixed yours up with that other little boy's. He had a pair just like yours in the end. I expect he is very upset, too. His trainers will be much too big!"

Mum phoned the little shoe shop and she was right. The other lady had rung just a few minutes before. Mum sorted it all out and then told Jack that they would go back tomorrow morning and this time he could put the right trainers on in the shop and walk home in them so there'd be no mistake.

Jack could hardly wait to go to bed so that the morning would come really quickly!

ODDSPOTS, the young leopard, was feeling tired as he lay along the branch of his favourite tree which overlooked the plains of Africa.

He was thinking of the chat he'd had with some swallows who'd perched on his tree on their way home from the north.

They'd told him a lot about the birds and animals who lived in the cold countries. They told him the amazing fact that some animals slept right through the winter weather.

Oddspot's Hibernation

He'd found out that this was called hibernation.

"This hot spell is very wearisome," Oddspot said to himself. "I think I'll hibernate. The sleep might do me good." He yawned and was soon fast asleep.

"Hurrooo! Hurrooo!"

Oddspot nearly fell off his branch in surprise. He rubbed his eyes and looked to see where the noise was coming from.

"Hurrooo!" an elephant trumpeted. "Excuse me, is this the tree that the elephants usually meet under?"

"No, it's not," Oddspot replied. "It's down by the waterhole."

Oddspot nodded off again, hoping that no more

absent-minded elephants would wander by.

"Crunch! Munch! Scrunch!"

Oddspot looked up blearily to see a giraffe.

"Hoi!" Oddspot said. "You've woken me up and you've eaten the leaves off the branch which gives me a nice shady patch! I can't hibernate in half a tree!"

"Hibernating?" The giraffe mused between mouthfuls. "Wait until I tell the others. They'll be so interested."

All the giraffes gathered around and Oddspot told them all about hibernating.

Once Oddspot had found another tree with more shade, he decided if he was to hibernate at all, he would need to avoid all these interruptions.

He made himself a smart sign which read Hibernating leopard. Please do not disturb! Oddspot had just drifted off to sleep when he was woken up again!

"Hibernating leopard?" a rhino declared in a loud voice. "What's a hibernating leopard? The only leopards I ever saw were spotty. Now, what else does that sign say?"

"It says, Please do not disturb!" Oddspot

said to the rhino in a somewhat sleepy voice.

"I'm trying to hibernate. It's a kind of long sleep, very popular with lots of animals, according to the swallows."

"Oh! Really!" the rhino replied. "I might try it. It sounds very restful." So, the rhino settled down below the tree and Oddspot climbed back up.

"Snooorrreee! Snnnooorrreee!" the rhino snored. Oddspot sat with his paws over his ears.

"It's just as well rhinos don't hibernate," he said to himself. "With all that snoring they would wake each other up!"

ODDSPOT set off to find another tree, well away from forgetful elephants, hungry giraffes and snoring rhinos.

After some searching Oddspot found another tree. He climbed up to a comfy branch and went to sleep.

"Squawk! Squawk! Squawk!"

Oddspot woke up, very startled.

"Quiet, please! I'm hibernating!" he roared.

"Don't you roar at me!" Mrs Hornbill squawked.

"Sorry," Oddspot said. "I'm trying to sleep."

"Sleep?" Mrs Hornbill screeched. "At this time of day? I can't creep about to suit sleepyheads. I've got the nest to tidy and the dinner to fetch!" All the other hornbills squawked in agreement.

Oddspot heard an odd rumbling sound. It was his tummy. He was very hungry.

After he'd had his tea he felt a lot better.

"I don't think I'll hibernate any more." He yawned. "It's far too tiring. Between explanations and tramping about looking for trees I'm worn out. I think I'll have an after-tea nap."

With that he dozed off happily to catch up on all the sleep he'd missed while he was trying to hibernate!

DO NOT DISTURB!

41

Back To School

42

SALLY was spending the day with her big cousin, Joanna.

"I'm going back to school next week," Joanna said.

"Oh, dear." Sally spoke sadly. "Then I'll have nobody to play with. I wish I was old enough to go to school with you."

Just then Aunt Sarah called them.

"Come and get ready, girls. We're going to the shops."

Joanna and Sally hurried downstairs.

"We're going to get all the things Joanna needs for school," Aunt Sarah said.

They drove to town.

"First we'll buy your school uniform, Joanna," Aunt Sarah decided. "You've grown too big for what you wore last year."

They chose a grey skirt and matching sweater with the school badge on it. Joanna tried on the clothes and looked very smart. Sally wished she could have a school uniform.

Joanna needed new shoes. The first pair she tried on pinched her toes.

"No use," Aunt Sarah said. "You must have a bigger size."

The second pair had laces and Joanna thought she'd like a big shiny buckle instead.

"Ah," the shop lady said, smiling. "We have just what you want."

She fetched a pair with bright buckles to fasten them.

"Thank you," Joanna said. "They're just right."

The next shop they went to sold pencils.

"You may each choose six pencils for writing and four for colouring," Aunt Sarah told Sally and Joanna.

The girls chose the prettiest pencils they could find to write with, then one red, one blue, one yellow and one green for colouring.

"Now we'll need pencil cases to put the pencils in," Aunt Sarah said. Joanna chose a blue case and Sally chose a pink one.

"Do we have to get anything more?" Joanna asked.

"One more thing," Aunt Sarah said. "Are you tired?"

"My legs are a bit tired," Sally admitted.

"Then let's go into this café and have some ice-cream."

READY to go on?" Aunt Sarah asked when they'd finished their ice-creams.

"Yes," the girls said. "Where are we going next?"

"To get a bag for you, Joanna. You need something to carry your books in."

Joanna took quite a long time to choose a school bag as there were so many in the shop.

Sally knew at once which one she'd choose if she was going to school. It was a pink bag with a picture of a little blue rabbit on it. How she wished she could go to school with the pink bag on her shoulder.

At last Joanna chose one — a blue bag to match her pencil case.

"Time for us to take you home, Sally," Aunt Sarah said.

"Look what I've got!" Sally shouted to her mummy when she got home. "A new pencil case. I think I'll keep it till I go to school."

"Well, that won't be long," Mummy told her. "A nursery school is starting next week in the village and you're going to go to it."

"Yes," Daddy added, "so I've bought you a school bag to carry your pencil case in."

He went to fetch the bag. And it was the pink one with the picture of the little blue rabbit on it.

"Oh, I'm ever so happy!" Sally said with a big smile and she gave both Mummy and Daddy a hug.

43

Always At Home

SAMMY THE SNAIL slid very slippety-slowly round the garden one night, enjoying a stroll in the white moonlight.

"Wherever I roam, I'm always at home," he said happily.

Just then he met Archie Ant.

"Poor Sammy Snail," Archie Ant said. "It just doesn't seem fair, you have to carry your home everywhere."

Sammy Snail thought for a long time.

"You're right," he said at last. "Please may I come and live with you instead?"

"The more the merrier!" Archie Ant said.

Sammy Snail tried to squeeze into Archie Ant's underground home. He tried again and again, but he couldn't do it. Sadly he slid away.

Soon he met Selina Slug.

"Poor Sammy Snail!" she said. "It just doesn't seem fair, you have to carry your home everywhere."

Sammy Snail thought for a long time.

"You're right!" he said at last. "Please may I come and live with you instead?"

"Be my guest," Selina Slug said.

Sammy Snail tried to squeeze into Selina Slug's home under a stone. He tried again and again, but he couldn't do it. Sadly he slid away.

Before long he met Millie Moth.

"Poor Sammy Snail," she said. "It just doesn't seem fair, you have to carry your home everywhere."

Sammy Snail thought for a long time.

"You're right," he said. "Please may I come and live with you instead?"

"Feel free," Millie Moth said.

Sammy Snail tried to squeeze into Millie Moth's home in a crack in a tree-trunk. He tried again and again, but he couldn't do it.

"I'll have to carry my home everywhere after all," he said with a sigh.

JUST then he felt a raindrop — then two drops — then more.

"It's going to pour!" Archie Ant cried. "Hurry home everyone!"

Quick as a tick Sammy Snail curled up tight in his shell.

The others hurried home as fast as they could, but Archie Ant got wet feet and knees. Selina Slug fell in a puddle up to her middle and Millie Moth was splashed with drips from the trees.

At last it stopped raining. The moon shone out again.

Sammy Snail came out of his shell. He hadn't got wet at all.

"I want to fly in the moonbeams high," Millie Moth said. "But first I must get my wings dry."

"I want to have fun and roll and tumble," Selina Slug said. "But first I must climb out of this puddle."

"I want to look for something to eat," Archie Ant said. "But first I must dry my knees and feet."

"Poor Archie Ant! Poor Selina Slug! Poor Millie Moth!" Sammy Snail said. "They got caught in the rain on their way home. I kept dry all the time in my shell home."

He slid slippety-slowly, round the garden enjoying a stroll in the white moonlight.

"Wherever I roam, I'm always at home," he said happily and he never tried to move home again.

45

Lauren's Lunch

"I'M making your packed lunch for school," Lauren's mummy called out one morning. "What would you like?"

"Cheese and pickle sandwiches, please," Lauren said as usual.

Lauren ate cheese and pickle sandwiches every day. In fact, she never ate much else at home, either! She just didn't like other foods.

"Are you sure you wouldn't like a change?" Lauren's mummy asked hopefully. "I've some lovely sliced beef and fresh tomatoes. Why not try some?"

"No, thank you, Mummy," Lauren replied. "I hate tomatoes. I'll just have my favourite cheese and pickle!"

Lauren's mummy sighed as she packed the pretty pink lunchbox Lauren always took with her to school.

"Time we were leaving," she called. "We'd better hurry or we'll miss our bus!"

When they arrived outside the school gates, Lauren's mummy kissed her goodbye. As Lauren skipped inside, she noticed a gorgeous little

kitten sitting by the fence.

"Hello, Kitty!" She smiled and couldn't resist giving the kitten a cuddle.

Then she rushed inside.

At lunchtime Lauren had a shock. Her lunchbox had gone missing!

"I can't find it anywhere!" she cried. "Where have I left it?"

Her friend, Charlotte, tried to help.

"Do you remember bringing it with you from home?" she asked.

Lauren thought hard.

"Yes," she replied. "I must have. Oh, where is it?"

Charlotte and two other classmates, Mark and Stacey, searched the desks and shelves, but they found nothing.

"Let's tell Miss Collins," Mark suggested.

When Miss Collins, their teacher, heard about the missing lunchbox she also started looking, but it had vanished into thin air!

By now, Lauren was beginning to feel hungry.

"I wish I could eat one of my cheese and pickle sandwiches right now!" She sighed.

Miss Collins smiled.

"I don't have anything with cheese or pickle in it," she told Lauren kindly. "But I did some

early shopping before coming to school. You can have one of these meat pies."

Miss Collins handed her the pie.

"Thank you," Lauren said politely, though she was certain it wouldn't taste nice!

Charlotte pressed a little wrapped parcel into Lauren's hand.

"My mummy always gives me far too much food." She smiled. "Try this — it's a slice of quiche."

As Lauren nodded her thanks, Mark thrust a cake in her other hand.

"It's carrot cake." Mark sighed. "My favourite!"

Carrot cake? Lauren gulped. Now she had a whole lapful of food and she didn't like the sound of any of it. If only she hadn't lost her lunchbox!

SHE didn't know what to do. She didn't want to look ungrateful and her tummy was rumbling. So, carefully, she took a small bite of Charlotte's quiche. It had funny bits of red in it. Lauren hoped they weren't tomato.

To her surprise, it tasted delicious!

"Mmm!" Lauren smiled. "Are these red bits peppers?"

"No — tomato!" Charlotte told her.

Lauren tried Miss Collins' pie next. That tasted really good, too. In fact, all the food was lovely. Lauren was quite sad when it was all gone!

The rest of the day passed quickly and soon it was home time. Lauren ran out of the building to say hello to her mummy who was waiting by the gate. Then she stopped in surprise. By the fence was her pink lunchbox!

"Of course!" Lauren giggled. "I put my lunchbox down when I cuddled that kitten this morning!"

Lauren's mummy was very amused to hear about her unusual lunch. And she pretended to faint with shock when Lauren asked if she could have something different in her lunchbox the next day!

"Mummy," Lauren added with a big smile on her face, "can we go to the park now to feed the ducks?"

Can you guess what those lucky ducks had to eat? Yes, you're right! Lauren's cheese and pickle sandwiches, of course!

"HERE'S your present,
Kevin," Grandma
said, handing him a
gaily wrapped box.
"Now mind and don't
open it until your birthday."

It was the holidays and Kevin was
spending them at his grandma's house.

"I love it here," he exclaimed
suddenly, running up and down in the
garden and flapping his arms around
like a goose.

"But you'll be glad to get home
again, too," Grandma said with a
laugh. "Don't you miss everyone?"

Kevin stayed deep in thought for a
moment, as if this was not an easy
question to answer.

"Yes," he said at last. "But . . ."

"But what?"

Grandma sat down and poured

The
Best
Present
Ever

them both another large glass of lemonade.

She had a good idea what the problem was. Kevin's family were living in quite a cramped little house and he had to share a bedroom with his brother.

"I'd like a room of my very own," he told her with great longing.

"Or if the garden was bigger . . ." he puckered out his lower lip and frowned ". . . I could maybe get a tent!"

Kevin's eyes brightened at the thought.

But the garden was very small indeed and the only attractive part about it was a rather nice sugar maple tree.

"We all need our own space," Grandma agreed. "But don't give up hope yet, Kevin. I'm sure something will turn up!"

Kevin thought that she winked at him. It was as if she knew something that he didn't.

"Are we moving to another house?" he asked.

But Grandma shook her head and kept on smiling in that same secretive way.

"Well, if we're not moving to another house, I'm never going to get a room of my own," he declared. "Unless they're going to build one on the top?"

But once again his grandma just shook her head and laughed.

"No, I'm afraid not," she replied and started busying herself in the kitchen, for soon it would be time for supper.

It felt good to be home, even if it was crowded and everyone seemed to be milling around and talking at once.

"Happy birthday," Kevin's sisters yelled and they all gathered round to watch him blow out the candles on his cake.

Kevin saw at once that his family had that same air of mystery and excitement about them as Grandma. What was going on?

He opened his presents and tucked into a slice of birthday cake, catching his mother's eye when she came in with a fresh jug of lemonade.

"Where's Dad?" he asked, licking icing off his fingers and being careful not to get any on his clothes.

"He's adding the finishing touches to your present," she told him. "He's out in the garden. Why don't you go out there and see for yourself?"

Kevin knew that all the odd behaviour he'd seen over the past few days, first with his grandma and now with the rest of his family, must have something to do with this mysterious gift.

Mum said it was in the garden, which meant that it must be something big — like maybe a basketball hoop, or a new bicycle?

KEVIN sped out the back door with his family following excitedly behind him.

And there it was. The very first thing he saw as he opened the back door was the loveliest little house imaginable, tucked up into the branches of the sugar maple tree.

It was a tree-house!

"Happy birthday, son," Dad said. "A little place of your very own."

"This is the very best birthday present ever," Kevin cried happily. "Thank you . . . thank you!"

Then he hugged everyone and invited them all up the ladder, one at a time, to see his very own house.

49

Katie's Special Friend

KATIE is a little girl
A lot like many others.
She hasn't any sisters and
She hasn't any brothers.

At school she has a lot of friends,
But when it's time for home,
Since Katie's house is out of town
She often plays alone.

In her garden by herself,
Sighed Katie, one fine day,
"I wish, I wish, I really wish
Someone would come to play!"

Just then, she heard a tiny voice
Say, "Katie, play with me!"
To her surprise, a fairy stood
There, pretty as could be.

This was the only fairy
That Katie had ever seen.
Said Katie, "You're so beautiful,
Are you a Fairy Queen?"

The fairy laughed. "Oh, no, I'm just
A young girl like yourself!
At home I have a brother
And he's a little elf."

Katie and the fairy girl
Had so much fun that day.
When tea time came, the fairy said
She'd have to go away.

"Oh, please say that you'll come
again!"
Cried Katie in delight.
The fairy smiled as she replied,
"I do believe I might."

She placed a kiss on Katie's cheek
And flew away up high,
While Katie stood and watched, and
waved
Her fairy friend goodbye.

The fairy soon was out of sight
And Katie wondered then
Had it been real or just a dream —
And would she come again?

Since then the fairy's often been
To keep little Katie company.
So Katie's never lonely now,
The way she often used to be.

ACTIVITY

Can you imagine what a fairy would look like?
Draw your ideas here!

Harry The Hermit Crab

HARRY the hermit crab was the smallest out of all his friends and he didn't like it one bit!

"I wish I wasn't so little," Harry said to his mummy, sighing. "I have the tiniest shell in the sea. It looks really silly!"

"There's nothing wrong with being small," Harry's mummy replied. "Besides,

52

Harry, with only a little, lightweight shell to carry around you scuttle much faster than some of your friends!"

Harry knew that was true, but he still wanted to be bigger.

One sunny morning, Harry went exploring along the sandy bay. All of a sudden he spotted the biggest empty shell he had ever seen. It was beautiful!

"This shell is perfect!" Harry gasped. "If I wore this shell instead of my old tiny one I'd be the biggest hermit crab in the sea!"

Making up his mind he popped out of his little shell and tried the large one on for size.

"Phew – it's very heavy!" Harry gasped. "And terribly loose!"

Harry could hardly move! But then he noticed his reflection in a rock pool. He looked great!

That's it!" Harry laughed. "I'm keeping it!"

And he threw his old shell away and scuttled off slowly to show his friends his new look.

Sadly, however, Harry didn't get the reaction he was hoping for!

"Oh, Harry, you look ridiculous!" Lucy Limpet giggled.

"Where are you, Harry?" Walter Whelk joked. "I can hardly see you in that big shell!"

But Harry didn't care what his friends said. At last he felt big!

After wearing his new shell for a few hours, Harry felt rather tired. He decided to crawl back home and rest. But as he dragged himself along the shoreline something unexpected happened. A little girl was out collecting empty shells. She stopped and picked Harry up!

"What a beautiful big shell," the girl said. "I'll keep it!" Because Harry was so small, she didn't even see his little head popping out! She thought that the shell was no longer being used as anyone's home.

The little girl carried Harry up the beach in a bucket. Then he was poured out on to the sand, on top of a big pile of other empty shells of every shape and size!

"Hmm!" Harry said as the girl ran down to the shore to look for more treasures. "I'd better hurry and escape before she gets back!"

Poor Harry! His new shell was SO heavy he could hardly move more than a few steps at a time!

"What am I going to do?" Harry cried. "I wish I'd never moved into this great big shell!"

Harry glanced at the shell collection the girl had left on the sand.

SUDDENLY he spotted his own lovely little shell!

"Hurrah!" Harry cried. Quickly he slipped back into it and raced at top speed down to the water's edge. Phew! Harry soon found his friends again and he did enjoy telling everyone about his adventures.

"See, being small does have its uses!" Lucy Limpet grinned. "You're better off staying just as you are."

Harry smiled happily.

It would be nice, one day, to be big, he thought. But for now he was content to be little Harry, the smallest hermit crab in the sea!

53

"My word," Mummy said, looking at the calendar. "It's Shrove Tuesday - Pancake Day."

"Can we help you to make pancakes?" Duncan and Kirsty asked.

"Yes," Mummy said, "but let's look in the cupboard first and see if we've got everything we need to make them."

They looked in the cupboard and discovered they didn't have enough flour or eggs.

"I quite forgot about Pancake Day," Mummy said. "If I'd remembered I'd have put flour and eggs on our shopping list. Now we'll have to go to the supermarket and buy those things."

As they walked to the supermarket they met Mr and Mrs Jones from next door.

"Hello, what are you two doing today?" Mr Jones asked.

"We're going to buy flour and eggs so that we can make pancakes," Duncan said.

"You see, it's Pancake Day," Kirsty said.

"Lucky you," Mrs Jones said. "We're very fond of pancakes but we're too busy painting our kitchen to make any."

"It won't be a proper Pancake Day." Mr Jones sighed.

In the supermarket, they met Miss Park pushing her aunt in her wheelchair.

"Have you come for something nice?" Aunt Florence asked Duncan and Kirsty.

"Just flour and eggs," Duncan said.

"It's Pancake Day and we're going to make pancakes," Kirsty told her.

"How lovely." Aunt Florence smiled.

"You won't be able to make any for us Agnes," she said to Miss Park, "for you're helping at the flower festival in the church this afternoon, aren't you?"

"I'm afraid so," Miss Park said. "No pancakes for us today."

On the way home they caught up with Mrs Brown and her little boy, Toby, in his pram.

"Been shopping?" Mrs Brown asked.

"Yes, Mummy forgot today was Pancake Day and we had to go to the supermarket for flour and eggs," Kirsty said.

"Oh, dear," Mrs Brown said. "I quite forgot, too, and I've so much ironing to do I won't have time to make any."

When they reached home Duncan and Kirsty helped Mummy measure out all the things to make pancakes. Then Mummy cooked the pancakes on the stove and tried to toss some of them. Mummy wasn't very good at that but they had great fun watching her try. Duncan counted the pancakes as Mummy made them.

"We've made twenty pancakes," Duncan said, "but there're only four of us in our family."

"I thought we might have a pancake party," Mummy said. "Do you remember all the people we met today who weren't going to have pancakes?"

"Yes," the children said.

"And they all wished they could have some," Kirsty added.

"Well, let's invite them all along for tea and pancakes," Mummy said.

So Mummy phoned Mr and Mrs Jones, Miss Park and Aunt Florence, and Mrs Brown and Toby. They all said they'd love to come.

The children picked a posy of snowdrops out of the garden and Mummy put them in the centre of the table.

The visitors arrived when Daddy came home. Everybody had two pancakes each, even little Toby.

"We've had a lovely Pancake Day after all," they said. "Thank you for inviting us."

55

When The Kookaburra Laughs

IN the far, far away country of Australia there lived a little kangaroo called Joey. Joey's mother had a pouch. It was like a wonderful pocket where Joey could curl up safe and warm.

Joey and his mother belonged to a mob of kangaroos. The leader of the mob was an old man kangaroo called Big Red. Big Red was strong and brave. One day, Joey would be strong and brave like Big Red.

The summer had been hot. The rains hadn't come and the grass was brown and dry. In the tall gum trees, mother koalas slept with their babies clinging to their backs. Kangaroos rested in the shade, away from the scorching sun. Even the birds were quiet and still.

"When will the rain come?" Joey asked his mother. He had never seen rain, but Big Red had told him about it — about how it made the grass grow tender and green.

"The kookaburra knows," Mother Kangaroo told Joey. "When the kookaburra laughs, the rain will come."

But the kookaburra didn't laugh and the rain didn't come — not for a long time.

One day, Big Red stood up tall on his back legs and sniffed the air. The mob was hungry. Big Red would lead them to another place where there was grass to eat and water to drink.

Inside Mother Kangaroo's pouch, Joey slept. Suddenly he was jerked awake as his mother stood up and bounded away across the grass with the other kangaroos.

Mother Kangaroo could hop very fast. Joey could hear the thump, thump, thump and feel the bump, bump, bump of her big feet as she hopped through the bush.

On and on they went until they came to a wide open space where green grass grew and a wide river gurgled merrily past shady trees. There they stopped.

The kangaroos stayed by the river for many days and every day Joey grew bigger and stronger. There were many new and exciting things for a young kangaroo to learn.

Joey practised his hopping and when Big Red told Joey about danger and how to stay safe, Joey listened carefully.

THE mob was restless one day. They lifted their faces to sniff the air. A cool, gusty wind whispered in the treetops and stirred the dust and fallen leaves.

"The rain is coming," the kangaroos whispered to one another.

Joey knew it was so, for just then the kookaburra's laugh grew louder, echoing across the treetops and out over the hills. Other kookaburras joined in and soon the treetops rang with the sound of joyous laughter as the first big drops of rain began to fall.

Rain! Wonderful, cooling rain. It rained on the trees and the brown grass. It rained on Joey and trickled down his nose. And when the rain passed, the wet bush sparkled in the sunlight and everything was fresh and clean.

Not long after that day Joey had a surprise when he climbed into his mother's pouch. No matter now much he wriggled and jiggled, his head or his feet stuck out! He had grown too big for Mother Kangaroo's pouch.

Now, when Big Red bounds away across the grass, the young kangaroo is always at his side. One day, Joey will be strong and brave — just like Big Red, the leader of the mob.

Perhaps, one day, the little kangaroo will lead his own mob through the bush to where the grass is tender and green.

Jake's Special Sailor Suit

"GREAT news!" Jake and Chloe's mum said when she collected them both from school. "Auntie Lisa is getting married! Chloe, she'd like you to be her bridesmaid.

Chloe did an excited twirl! She'd always wanted to be a bridesmaid!

"Will I wear a pink dress with ribbons?" she cried eagerly.

Her mum laughed.

"I don't know what colour the dress will be," she said. "I'm sure you will look very pretty in it, though."

Then their mum looked at Jake.

"Auntie Lisa is choosing you a lovely outfit, too." She smiled. "She wants you to be her pageboy."

Jake frowned. He wasn't sure he wanted to be a pageboy. He remembered his best friend Andy saying that when he'd been a pageboy last year, his job was to carry the bride's long train. Poor Andy had nearly tripped over it twice! And he'd had to wear funny clothes.

A few weeks before the wedding, a big parcel arrived in the post. It was Chloe and Jake's wedding outfits.

Chloe couldn't wait to try her dress on. It was pale blue with tiny flowers sewn on to the straps.

"Ooooh, it's beautiful!" she cried happily. "Jake, come and show me yours!"

Jake came downstairs very slowly. Auntie Lisa had chosen a sailor's outfit for him, with a matching hat.

"You look very handsome," his mum said.

"I feel stupid!" Jake scowled.

"Cheer up, Jake. You've always liked boats," his dad said. "I think you both look very nice."

AT last the big day arrived. It was a lovely morning and the family drove down to the coast where the wedding was being held. Everything went well and Jake didn't trip up or forget anything. And he was very surprised to find out that Auntie Lisa had married a sailor!

"That's why I wanted you to wear this outfit," Auntie Lisa whispered to Jake.

After the wedding, Jake had an even bigger surprise. They were holding the wedding party on a huge boat!

"Look, Dad!" Jake gasped. "There are real sailors here dressed just like me!"

"I bet you don't feel so silly now." His dad smiled.

Jake grinned – he didn't!

Auntie Lisa's new husband came over.

"How would you like to meet the captain and look around the boat's bridge, Jake?" he asked. "It's not normally allowed, but as you're dressed for the part I'm sure the captain wouldn't mind."

Jake had a super time. The captain and other sailors showed him round the engine room and below deck.

ALL too soon, the wedding day was over.

"Did you enjoy yourselves?" the children's mum asked on the way home.

"It was lovely!" Chloe sighed.

"What about you, Jake?" Mum asked, though she already knew the answer.

Jake grinned and straightened his sailor's hat.

"I've made a very important decision," he said. "When I grow up, I want to be a sailor!"

Little **Blue** **School** Bus

TOOT! TOOT! TOOT! The little blue school bus stopped outside the school gate where the children were waiting. "All aboard for Nursery Rhyme Land," Mr Duncan, the driver, said cheerily. "First stop the magic castle, then on to see Humpty Dumpty and Little Miss Muffet."

Mr Duncan said the same thing every afternoon as the boys and girls climbed aboard the little blue school bus for the ride home. He did it to make the children giggle.

But today, no-one giggled. The children were sad. Today was the last time they would ride in the little blue school bus.

The little bus was old. It rattled and wheezed as it went up and down the streets. Its paint was scratched and faded, and the seats were all lumpy and bumpy.

"It shakes so much I'm afraid the wheels might fall off one day," Mr Duncan told the children. "The little blue school bus needs a rest."

The next morning Mr Duncan was driving a shiny red school bus. It was very smart — there was carpet on the floor and the seats were soft and very springy.

"All aboard for Nursery Rhyme Land," Mr Duncan called cheerily. "First stop the magic castle, then on to see Jack and Jill and the cow that jumped over the moon."

The children giggled as they climbed aboard and tried the soft, springy seats. They looked out of the wide windows as the red bus went up and down the streets without one rattle or wheeze.

After a while the children forgot about the little blue school bus, until one day, there it was, parked in the school playground.

"Why is the little blue school bus here?" the children asked their teacher, but she only smiled and told them to wait and see.

One day a truck came with workmen and ladders and boxes of tools. The workmen climbed all over the little school bus. They scraped off all the old paint. They pulled out the lumpy, bumpy seats. The next day they came with pots of paint.

When the children came out to play, they stood and stared — the little blue school bus had a new coat of shiny blue paint.

"Tomorrow is painting day," the teacher said. "Bring an old shirt — a big daddy-sized shirt."

"What are we going to paint?" the boys and girls asked the next morning when they were dressed in their shirts. "Where is the paper?"

"We don't need any paper," their teacher said. She was smiling as though she knew a secret. "Bring your paints and follow me."

The teacher took the children outside. She took them to the little school bus with its coat of shiny blue paint. And what do you think they did then?

They painted big yellow daisies with smiley faces along the sides of the little blue bus. They painted butterflies and birds and fluffy, white clouds. Then they painted a big, yellow sun with a happy face. How grand the little blue school bus looked!

But the little blue school bus wasn't finished yet — there was still the inside of the bus to finish. The workmen put down a fluffy red carpet and, instead of new seats, they brought in lots of beanbags and big cushions.

THE little blue school bus with the yellow daisies and butterflies, the birds and fluffy clouds and the smiley sun, became the children's special place. There were boxes of toys to play with and story books to read. But the best thing of all was pretending to be Mr Duncan driving the little blue school bus up and down pretend streets.

Toot! Toot! Toot! All aboard for Nursery Rhyme Land. First stop the magic castle, then on to see Humpty Dumpty and Little Bo Peep.

Toot! Toot! Toot! The little blue school bus went up and down the streets without one rattle or wheeze.

Come To My Party

PLEASE come to my party
It's happening just down the street.
We'll have contests and games
And then we'll sit down
To have lots of nice things to eat.

Mum's giving a prize
I don't know exactly what.
But she says she is sure that the winner
Will really like it a lot.

Mum's making the sandwiches.
There will be egg, chicken and ham.
But do you know I think I'd much rather have
A sandwich with strawberry jam!

My gran is coming to join us.
And she just loves to bake.
She's promised she's going to make me
A fabulous fireworks cake!

Mum's made lots of red jelly,
It's jiggling and wriggling and squiggling.
And every time I look at it
I just can't stop myself giggling.

My dad's done the balloons
They're huge - the biggest in town.
But I really, really wish
We could have hired a clown.

I'll say thank you for coming
When the party is done.
Don't you agree that bonfire night
Is such a great deal of fun?

ACTIVITY

use this space to draw some of the things mentioned in the poem, like a fireworks cake!

DINO'S DECISION

DINO the donkey had been a favourite of all the children on Barnaby Beach for many years. They loved sitting on his back and riding along the beach, and they loved Dino, too.

Although Dino loved all the children he felt that perhaps it was time he had a change, so he decided to look for somewhere else to spend next summer.

One afternoon Farmer Fernando left the big gate to his field open. When no-one was looking, Dino trotted out into the outside world.

"Now I can go wherever I want!" Dino told himself happily.

In one of the many fields he passed by, Dino noticed Old Dylan Donkey.

"I need a change," Dino explained. "I'm looking for somewhere quiet and peaceful to spend next summer."

"Well, it's very quiet and peaceful in this field," Old Dylan Donkey brayed. "There's plenty of room for you, too."

So Dino decided to stay in the field with Old Dylan Donkey. By late afternoon, though, Old Dylan Donkey fell fast asleep and he didn't wake up until the next morning!

"It's too quiet and peaceful here for me," Dino said as soon as Old Dylan Donkey opened his eyes.

But Old Dylan Donkey simply closed his eyes again, then carried on sleeping once more!

Dino left him and continued on his way until he reached a little village.

It was Market Day and Dino had never been to a market before. Mr Burns, the baker, saw him.

"A donkey's just what I need to take my special rolls and fancy cakes to the market," he told Dino. "You see, my car has broken down and needs repairing."

Being needed made Dino feel quite important.

Before you could say "yummy cream cakes", Dino found himself pulling a cart load of rolls and cakes.

"You can take my sweets and chocolates to market for me at the same time," the owner of the sweet shop called to Dino, "I've a lot to do today."

After that, the greengrocer loaded the cart high with fruit and vegetables and even Mrs Blossom the florist put flowerpots and bunches of flowers on the cart, too.

IT seemed that all the shopkeepers had something for Dino to take to the market! Not one of them realised that Dino had never been on a busy road before and wasn't used to all the traffic. When someone sounded his horn Dino almost jumped with fright.

Luckily, he soon reached the market place and his work was finished. Someone gave him a nice big carrot to thank him for all his help.

After he'd munched the carrot, Dino thought that the best thing to do would be to return to Farmer Fernando's field while he decided where to go next summer.

He knew now that pulling a cart would be too difficult for him during the hot summer months.

He knew he hated being in noisy traffic.

He knew, too, that being in a field with only Old Dylan Donkey for company would be very boring and much too quiet.

So, where did Dino decide he'd go next summer?

Well, there really was only one place where he knew he'd definitely be happy and that was back on Barnaby Beach with all the children who loved him so much. You see, Dino didn't really need a change after all!

Jonathan's Saucepan

JONATHAN was playing in the garden while his mum cleaned out her kitchen cupboards. "Would you like this old saucepan to play with?" his mum asked. "I'm throwing it away."

"Oh, yes, please!"

Jonathan had thought of a plan for a game. He put the saucepan on the path and gathered up some pebbles. Then he tried to toss the stones into the pan. When he managed to get one in it made such a clatter! It was a great game.

After a while, Jonathan tried to think of another game to play with the saucepan. He fetched the little spade that his dad had bought for him so that he could help when there were plants to be set or weeds to be dug up.

Jonathan used the spade to dig in the soft soil and soon he had filled the saucepan to the top. He patted down the soil, just the way he did when he built sandcastles on the beach, and then he quickly turned the pan upside down and lifted it up. There was a lovely mud castle!

Jonathan decorated his castle with stones and leaves until it really looked grand. Then he tried to think of a new game to play with the pan.

He held up the saucepan by the handle and banged it with a stick. It made a great drum! Jonathan marched up and down and all around the garden, banging his drum as he went. He felt like a soldier, leading the band.

His mum came out into the garden and said it was time for lunch. She was surprised when Jonathan told her all the things he had thought of for games with the pan.

"I think I have an idea, too," she said. "You will need to dig a hole in the corner of the garden there."

Jonathan wondered what his mum's idea could be. He dug a hole with his spade as quickly as he could.

"Now put the saucepan into the hole."

Jonathan picked up the pan and placed it carefully into the hole so that only the rim and the long handle showed above the ground.

"That's perfect," Mum said. "Now, if we put in some water the birds will have a lovely bathtub to wash in."

JONATHAN fetched some water in a bucket.

"Put a big stone into the pan first," Mum told him. "Just in case any other creatures — like hedgehogs or frogs — fall in. Then they will be able to climb out again."

Jonathan found a big stone and put it into the saucepan. Then he poured in the water and the bird bath was ready.

While Jonathan and his mum ate their lunch they watched through the kitchen window. Before very long the birds found the pan of water and began splashing in it happily.

"What a lot of things that old saucepan has been today!" Mum laughed.

"Yes," Jonathan said happily, "and now the birds can play in it every day!"

ONE spring morning Daddy was just about to leave for work. "I bought some seeds for you to sow now it's spring time, but I can't remember where I put them," he said to Mummy and Denise.

"Never mind," Mummy said, "Denise and I will see if we can find them."

"They'll be in pretty paper packets," Mummy said. "Let's try looking first of all in the garden shed."

They looked on shelves and inside boxes and pots in the garden shed.

"They're not here," Mummy said when they'd had a good look round.

"Where shall we look next?" Denise asked.

"The greenhouse," Mummy said. "Take Daddy's small trowel with you, Denise."

"Why?" Denise asked.

"We'll need it to draw lines in the earth to put the seeds in," Mummy explained.

They searched everywhere in the greenhouse. Mummy put some water in the watering-can and let Denise give some of Daddy's plants a drink.

"We'll need the watering-can, too, when we've sown the seeds," Mummy said.

"Where has Daddy left the seeds?" Denise wondered.

"I think we'll look in the garage next," Mummy said. Daddy had been sawing up logs in the garage.

"Maybe the seeds fell out of Daddy's pocket," Denise suggested.

"Perhaps," Mummy said. "Let's look among the logs." Denise helped Mummy to lift logs and look underneath them, but they found no seeds.

"No luck I'm afraid," Mummy said. "Let's look on Daddy's work-bench." But the work-bench was bare except for a hammer and a few nails.

"Shall I tidy Daddy's nails for him?" Denise asked.

"If you know where he keeps them," Mummy said.

"I know," Denise said and she opened the cupboard beneath the work-bench and lifted out a big tin box. "What a heavy box!" she said.

"Maybe the seeds are in it." Mummy helped Denise to open the tight lid, but the box had only nails inside.

WHEN Daddy came home Denise told him they hadn't found the seeds.

"I am sorry about that," Daddy said, "for I know you like doing things in the garden. Perhaps you'd like to come and help me with a few little gardening jobs before bedtime?"

"I would," Denise said. Daddy lifted his gardening jacket off its peg.

"Will you hold this for a minute, Denise?" he asked. But Denise accidentally let Daddy's coat fall to the floor. As it fell, some little packets slipped out of one of its pockets.

"There they are!" Mummy cried and she picked up the packets. "Here are the seeds, Denise. We'll be able to sow them after all."

"If you look at the pictures on the packets you'll see the flowers that will grow in the summer," Daddy explained.

"What a pretty garden we're going to have," Denise said as she looked at the flower pictures. "I can't wait for summer."

A Mouse's

Adventure

ONE day a little mouse called Pip decided to go exploring. He had never been exploring before. In fact, Pip had never even left home before. He lived with his mummy and daddy and brothers and sisters in the garden, under the old shed. He was a timid, shy mouse and not very adventurous.

While his brothers and sisters had all ventured out from the shed, Pip had stayed at home with his mummy.

Of course, he had heard all about the outside world from his family but he had never felt brave enough to find out what it was like for himself. But today Pip was not afraid. It was time to see what lay beyond the old garden shed.

And so, after saying goodbye to everyone, he peeped his nose outside. Goodness, everything was so very bright! Pip looked up. What was that? Blue. It must be the sky. He had heard all about the sky from his brother Toots.

He looked ahead. What was that? Green. It must be the grass. Pip had heard all about the grass from his sister Dot. He took a few hurried steps and found himself surrounded by hundreds of flowers of every colour and description. He had heard all about the flowers from his mummy. But he had never imagined how beautiful they would be.

Then quickly darting through the grass, Pip almost bumped into something. What was it? A small creature bobbed and hopped and said hello.

"Are you a bird?" asked Pip who had heard all about the birds from his sister Itzy.

"I am indeed," replied the sparrow. "And who are you?"

"I'm Pip, the garden shed mouse. I've never left home before and I've already come such a long way. All the way from there to here. How far have you been adventuring today Mr Sparrow?"

"All the way from here to the blue sky and beyond," replied the sparrow who at that moment fluttered his wings and soared up and away until he was quite out of sight.

Then all of a sudden Pip got a very big surprise indeed. He saw something that he had heard all about but had never expected to see so soon.

He looked up and up and up. It was a Big One! Mice were supposed to be frightened of Big Ones and Big Ones were supposed to be frightened of mice. But Pip wasn't scared. Neither was the Big One, a young girl called Jenny. Instead she sat down on the grass and gently stroked Pip's soft fur.

With his twinkly black eyes, delicate whiskers and tiny feet Jenny thought he was the cutest creature she had ever seen. Pip thought Jenny was nice too and not at all scary. He couldn't help feeling proud of himself. He was, after all, the only one from his family to meet a Big One and not run away.

Pip was having such fun playing outdoors, it was some time before he noticed the sun was going down. It was growing dark.

This must be the evening. He had heard all about the evening from Daddy. He remembered too that Daddy said all mice should be tucked up in bed before night-time.

So Pip hopped and ran and skipped until the garden shed came in sight. The world, he decided was a VERY BIG place and he would enjoy it again tomorrow and the day after.

He would chat to the sparrow and smell the lovely flowers and meet his new friend Jenny.

All the same, as Pip was welcomed back from his travels by his family he realised that what they had always told him was true – there really was no place like home.

71

Harry Hippo's Holiday

HARRY HIPPO sat sunbathing in the mud by a river in Africa with his mummy and little sister, Hannah.

"I'm bored," Harry said. "I wish I could go on holiday."

"Why do you want to go on holiday?" his mummy asked. "This is a lovely sunny place. It's the best in the whole wide world."

"I'm tired of playing in the mud. I want some adventure."

"Well, I think that's just silly," said Hannah. "Mud and sunshine are all I need. Do you want to play Splash-in-the-mud, Harry?"

"No, I've done that lots of times," Harry grumbled. "I want to play different games — on holiday."

"Well, why don't you go exploring up the river?" his mummy suggested. "I'll pack some lunch for you."

"That's a brilliant idea! I'll go exploring just for the day," Harry said.

"Remember to come back for tea!" his mummy called as Harry set off on his holiday.

Harry Hippo put his packed lunch in his back-pack and set off up the riverbank.

After a while he sat down to eat his lunch. Suddenly he heard a screeching noise.

A big golden monkey was sitting in a tree, waving his long, black tail. Two other monkeys scrambled along the branch to join him.

"Hello, Hippo!" they screeched. "Would you like to play Tig with us?"

"I'd love to," Harry said as he finished his sandwich.

"Follow us," the monkey said. "We're playing Tree Tig, leaping through the trees."

The monkeys screeched and leapt away through the trees but Harry couldn't keep up with them. He was thirsty, so he drank his bottle of juice.

AFTER he'd finished his lunch, he strolled through the trees and came out on the grassy plain.

Peering through the long grass, Harry saw some black and white striped animals, busy munching grass.

Harry wondered if they'd like to play with him and he ambled over to them.

"What's that?" One of the zebras whinnied. "Maybe it wants to eat us. Run for your lives!"

The zebra herd charged away across the savannah, kicking wildly.

Harry wandered across the plain until he came to a beautiful lake, full of pretty pink birds with long necks.

He ran down to the clear water to meet them.

"Would you like to come swimming with us?" the pink flamingos asked.

"I'd love to," Harry said and he dived in.

He splashed, chased and swam with the flamingos until he was tired out.

"I think I'd better go home now," he said to the flamingos.

"Bye, bye, Harry Hippo," they squawked.

HE wandered over the grassy plain, through the trees and back to the riverbank. Then he dived into the deep, muddy river and swam home.

"You're home just in time for your tea!" His mummy smiled.

"Did you enjoy your holiday?" Hannah asked.

"Yes! I met some monkeys and some zebras," Harry replied. "But the best was swimming with the pink flamingos."

"And which is better — home or holiday?" his mummy asked.

"Home's the best place in the world," Harry exclaimed. "Mud and sunshine are all I need. Let's play Splash-in-the-mud, Hannah!"

73

Peter In The Snow

PETER Polar Bear had soft white fur and blue eyes like sapphires. He sat on a shelf in a toy shop called Hickory Corner.

One day in winter, Sailor Ted, who sat next to Peter, said, "I think it's going to snow!"

"Snow? What's snow?" Peter asked.

"Snow is white," Sailor Ted said.

Peter shuffled along the shelf until he was next to Clementine, the clown doll.

"Clementine, what's snow?"

"Snow is cold!" Clementine stood on her head and waved her big feet in the air.

Grey Elephant backed away from the waving feet.

"What's snow?" Peter asked.

"Snow is soft, I think," Grey Elephant said. "But we don't have it in my country."

"What's snow?" Peter asked the Spotted Dog.

"Snow is wet!" Spotted Dog said.

Blue Rabbit was at the very end of the shelf.

"What's snow?" Peter asked.

"Snow is hard," Blue Rabbit said.

"But Elephant said it was soft!"

"Yes, hard and soft!"

Peter was puzzled. It was all very confusing.

"BUT WHAT DOES SNOW LOOK LIKE?" he demanded.

"Like that!" Spotted Dog said, pointing to the window.

OUTSIDE, large flakes of snow were falling from the sky. The pavement was covered in white stuff and so was the red post box near Hickory Corner.

"That's snow? It's beautiful!" Peter said.

"You would say that!" Blue Rabbit snapped. "Polar Bears like snow!"

"Do they?" Peter felt wildly excited. He wanted to go out in the snow. Now!

In a flash he climbed on to a lower shelf, swung along the ladder of a toy fire engine and slid down a blue plastic slide to the shop door. No-one, not even Mr and Mrs Dock, who owned the shop, noticed Peter slip through the door into the white world.

"Brrrrrrrrrrr . . . snow IS cold!" Peter shivered as flakes clung to his fur and floated in his eyes.

HE hurried along so quickly that he slipped and landed upside-down in a snowdrift.

"Snow IS soft!" he thought, struggling to get right way up again.

Back on his feet he rubbed his cold, damp nose.

"Snow IS wet!"

He walked into the park. Two little boys were throwing snow balls. One missed and hit Peter.

"Ouch, snow IS hard!"

At the park, Peter had an awful fright.

"Help!" he yelled, and he ran and ran and ran all the way back to Hickory Corner.

"HELP!"

"Whatever's wrong?" Sailor Ted asked.

"I've seen a giant!" Peter gasped. "It was staring at me with big black eyes!"

"What?"

"It had a long orange nose and enormous teeth and a red hat and a stripey scarf!"

Sailor Ted chuckled.

"That was no giant! That was a snowman!"

All the toys laughed. Peter sat on his shelf feeling rather silly.

"Did you find out about snow?" Grey Elephant asked.

"Yes. Snow is white and cold and soft and hard and wet."

"Did you like it?"

"Not much," Peter said. "But then, I'm not a *REAL* polar bear!"

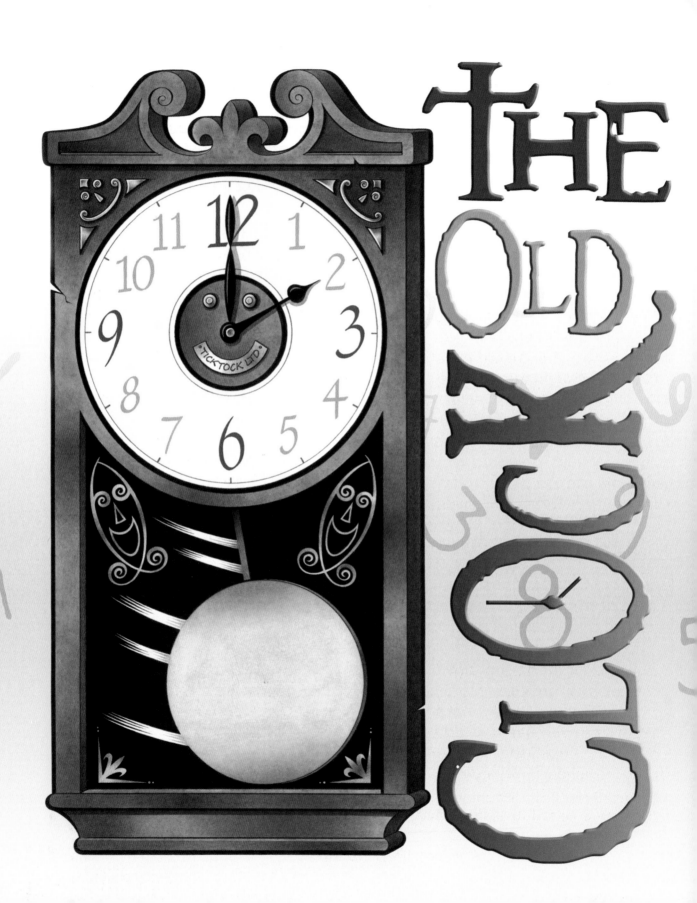

THE OLD CLOCK

THIS is Mr Arthur's old clock, Jamie," Dad said as he put the big brown parcel on the table.

"He's moving to a smaller house and he hasn't room for it. He asked me to take care of it." He took off the paper.

Jamie watched him. He was learning to tell the time. He looked at the round white face with the dark numbers.

The long, black hand was pointing to the twelve and the little one to the two. He knew that meant exactly two o'clock. That was an easy one.

"Isn't it a beauty, Jamie?" Dad said. "The case is real walnut like the big tree in our market square. Stroke it with your hand."

"It feels like the dining-room table when Mum polishes it," Jamie said. He put his ear close to the clock. "But it isn't ticking, Dad. Is it broken?"

"Oh, dear!" Dad sighed. "You're right. I don't think it liked being moved."

"I expect it misses being with Mr Arthur," Jamie said.

Dad turned the clock round and then reached for his tool box.

"I'll take the back cover off, Jamie," he said. "Then we'll see what's wrong."

Jamie was surprise to see all the wheels and cogs inside the case. Daddy attached a big round gold disc.

"That's called the pendulum," he said. "These small brass hammers make a chiming noise when they strike the quarter hours."

Jamie wished he could hear them.

"It needs your little fingers, Jamie," Dad said. "This spring has fallen off. Could you hold it for me?"

JAMIE picked it up carefully and Dad told him where to place it, right beside a tiny wheel.

Dad fixed the spring and the wheel together, although it was difficult with his big hands. Then Dad touched the pendulum gently and it began to swing to and fro, to and fro.

Jamie nearly jumped out of his skin as the small hammers began to strike. Boom! Boom! Boom! Three o'clock!

"It's working!" Jamie cried, clapping his hands. "The ticking is like Hickory, Dickory Dock."

"I don't want a mouse running up this clock!" Dad laughed. "Now, we'd better put some oil in just to make sure it all runs smoothly."

Dad went off to get his can from the shed.

Later, when Jamie was in bed, he listened to the clock chiming downstairs.

He was sure the clock would wake him up at eight o'clock. But, oh, dear, the clock forgot to chime. Well, that's what Jamie told his teacher when he was late for school. But perhaps he was just too sound asleep . . .

77

Strongbow The Calf

ROSE felt very proud this morning as she stood in the field. She had good reason to because she now had a beautiful calf lying beside her on the grass.

He had arrived only a few hours ago and was still shy and unsure of the world around him.

Rose bent over to touch his small warm body and gave him a gentle lick.

The calf felt much safer when he felt her rough tongue because he knew that she was there to protect him.

He felt especially brave when his mum nuzzled him like this. He tried again to stand up straight on his long wobbly legs. Another cow was standing near to Rose and the calf, she gave a soft mooing laugh when she saw how hopeless the calf was at standing up.

"Primrose doesn't understand," Rose said to her little calf. "She is too young to have a calf and she doesn't understand how proud I am of you."

Rose watched the young cow walk off swishing her tail and mooing again. She flicked her ears crossly. She would show Primrose just what a clever calf she had.

He wasn't having very much success at walking though. The little calf was really trying and he sang a song to himself to see if it would help him.

"My legs I think are much too long
Or else I'm doing something wrong.
Why is it that my front legs stand
But at the back in a heap I land?
It's not my fault I can't do it right
I think it's all to do with height!"

The calf fell down on the grass.

Rose thought that maybe he could do with a little help from her.

She pushed at his back legs with her nose so that they stood straight.

The calf was delighted. He lifted all his legs to walk — and fell flat on the ground!

Even Rose had to chuckle when she saw that.

"Never mind," she said. "Try again. But don't do it so fast this time. Watch me." She walked slowly forward and turned her head.

"Now you try," she said. The calf gave a mighty heave and lifted himself on to his legs.

"One leg at a time and slow.
That must be the way to go!"

The little calf tripped over and fell on his nose. He raised his sad brown eyes to his mother.

ROSE shook her head from side to side. He paused, took a deep breath and slowly tried again.

"Front right, back left.
It's easy now —
Front left, back right —
Once I learnt how.
Front right, back left —
It's simple now.
Front left, back right —
Walking like a cow."

He was very tired now after all his hard work. The little calf settled down beside his mother and fell asleep.

Rose licked his small furry head. He was a good little calf and he had learned his first important lesson.

She was so proud of her strong little calf and she knew a very good name to call him, she would call him Strongbow. Strongbow gave a big sigh. He was dreaming about walking.

"Right foot, left foot —
Stand up tall.
Left foot, right foot —
Now I won't fall."

79

Sam's Breakfast

BREAKFAST in bed, a special treat,
Sam thought was rather nice,
Until it all went sadly wrong –
He only tried it twice.

Cornflakes, tea and buttered toast,
He managed these with ease
Until the moment that he coughed
And then began to sneeze.
Oh, what a mess the sheets were in!
How cross his mummy got!
The cornflakes landed on his toes
And, oh, the tea was hot!

"Just be careful – don't choose eggs,"
Sam says. "I like them, too,
But if you kick about too much
They may end up on you!

"I chose an egg," Sam says, "because
It went so well with toast.
I took a book, as well, to read –
I blame the book the most!
It really was a funny book.
I read, and ate, and read
Until my laughter, jerking so,
Began to shake the bed.

"I couldn't help the laughing bit,
It really wasn't fair.
One moment all was well – and then
The tray was in the air!
The falling egg unyolked itself
And fell upon my nose.
The tea all splashed upon my face
And covered all my clothes.

"So now," Sam says, "in bed, don't eat!
But, if you do, please try
To keep the bed as still can be –
No need to ask me why!"

ACTIVITY

Why not try writing a poem about your favourite food. Remember, it doesn't have to rhyme!

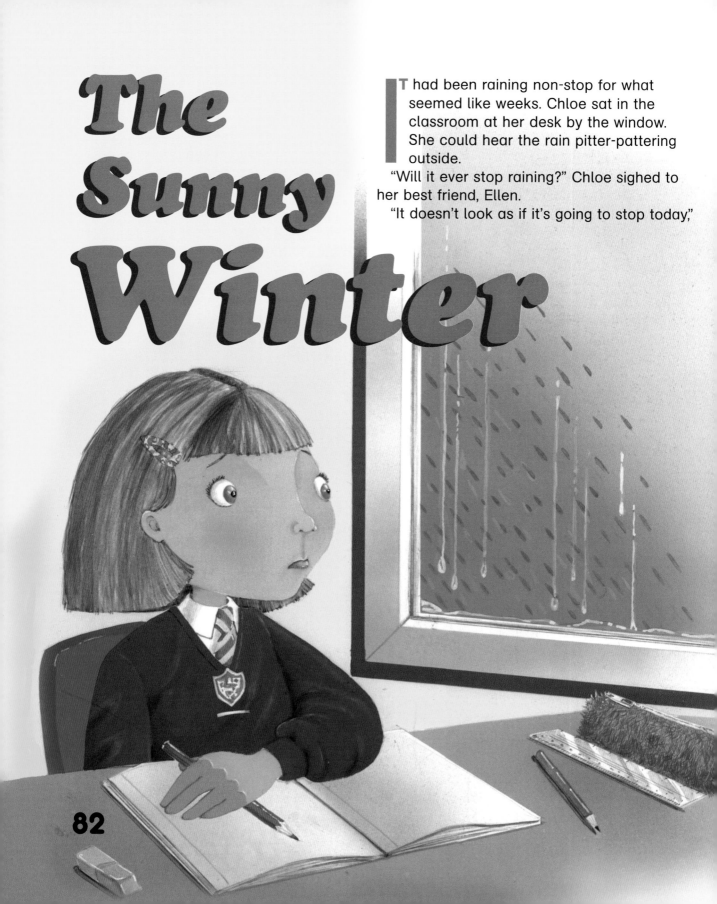

The Sunny Winter

T had been raining non-stop for what seemed like weeks. Chloe sat in the classroom at her desk by the window. She could hear the rain pitter-pattering outside.

"Will it ever stop raining?" Chloe sighed to her best friend, Ellen.

"It doesn't look as if it's going to stop today,"

said their teacher, Miss Willis. "I'm sorry, but you'll all have to stay inside the classroom again at break time. You'll get soaked if you play outside!"

The whole class groaned.

"How long is it till summer?" one boy, Archie, asked.

"Months!" Chloe replied. "If only we could bring it forward a bit."

Their first lesson that morning was art. Miss Willis was thoughtful as she handed out the paper and brushes.

"Let's cheer ourselves up and paint some pictures of the seaside," she told the class.

Soon everyone was busy drawing buckets and spades, sandcastles and shells, and pictures of themselves eating ice-creams! Chloe put her hand up.

"I don't know what to paint!" she said to Miss Willis.

"What do you miss most about summer?" Miss Willis asked her.

Chloe thought for a moment.

"The sun!" She laughed and she began to draw a picture of a bright shining sun!

At lunchtime it was still raining and Chloe and her friends had to stay indoors again.

So the class were quite happy when afternoon lessons began.

"Now, let's all try and remember our summer holidays last year!" Miss Willis said with a twinkle in her eye. "What did you all like doing most?"

EVERYONE had a story to tell. Ellen liked the puppet show. Archie loved building sandcastles and Chloe liked to look for crabs.

"Oh, if only we could wake up tomorrow and it would suddenly be summer again!" She sighed. The following morning when Chloe jumped out of bed it was still pouring with rain — AGAIN!

Quickly, Chloe got dressed and hurried down for breakfast. She still had to go to school.

Chloe met her friend Ellen in the corridor outside their classroom.

"The classroom door is locked!" Ellen told Chloe excitedly. "Miss Willis says we can't come in until she's finished preparing our surprise!"

Chloe giggled. She wondered what that surprise could be.

Just then, the door opened.

"You can all come in now!" Miss Willis said.

THERE were gasps of delight as the children trooped inside. Their teacher had hung the walls of their classroom with bright yellow and blue paper to look like a sandy beach and blue sea.

All their seaside paintings had been stuck up, too!

"Look!" Chloe cried. Her big golden sun was hanging from the ceiling!

"Oh, Miss Willis!" Ellen said. "It's really summery in here now. It looks just like the seaside!"

But Miss Willis had another surprise in store. Behind a curtain was hidden a small sandpit and a little stripy seaside puppet stall.

"These are just for use during playtime," Miss Willis explained. "I know how bored you've all been having to stay indoors because of the rain!"

The children couldn't wait to take it in turns to entertain their friends with a puppet show. And, of course, it would be great fun to build sandcastles.

"We didn't have to wait months for summer!" Chloe said happily. "In our classroom, it's already here!"

83

Lullaby For A Squirrel

ONE night, Baby Squirrel could not get to sleep. He tossed and turned in his cosy nest, high in a hole in the tree.

He shut his eyes and he counted to ten. He wasn't asleep so he counted again.

But it was no good. Baby Squirrel kept opening his eyes to look at the shining moon, the twinkling stars and the birds flying home.

"What shall I do?" he asked Big Sister Squirrel. "Look, I'm still wide awake! Will it soon be daybreak?"

"It won't be morning for ages," Big Sister Squirrel said. "But don't worry, I know how to send you to sleep."

She pulled funny faces and stood on her head. When that didn't work, she tried tickling instead.

But when she tickled his tummy with her bushy tail, Baby Squirrel only wriggled and giggled. He didn't give even the tiniest yawn.

"What shall I do?" he asked Daddy Squirrel. "Look, I'm still wide awake! Will it soon be daybreak?"

"It won't be morning for ages," Daddy Squirrel said.

"But don't worry. I know how to send you to sleep."

He ran up a tree and leapt from branch to branch, then rushed down head first, like an avalanche.

But Baby Squirrel didn't give even the tiniest yawn. Instead, he laughed so much he woke up all the other baby squirrels who lived in the tree.

"Is it a party?" they asked. "Can anyone come? Are there any nuts?"

They hurried to Baby Squirrel's home and before long everyone was chattering happily. They ate lots of nuts and had a competition to see how far they could throw the empty shells. Then they joined tails and danced along the branches, singing a jolly song.

Just then Mummy Squirrel appeared. She was surprised to see them up so late.

"Why aren't you all at home in your beds?" she asked. "At this hour you should be sleepyheads."

"I can't get to sleep," Baby Squirrel said. "Look, I'm still wide awake! Will it soon be daybreak?"

"It won't be for ages," Mummy Squirrel said. "But don't worry, I know how to send you to sleep."

She sat on a high branch so they could all see her.

"Are you sitting comfortably?" she asked. When everyone was quiet she began to sing a squirrel lullaby.

"The sun is setting in the west.
The little bird flies home to rest.
The squirrel's sleeping in his nest.
Sweet dreams to you —
the very best."

IT wasn't long before the baby squirrels began to yawn. They crept back to their nests and soon they were fast asleep.

"What about me?" Baby Squirrel cried. "Look, I'm still . . . wide . . . awake!"

He gave a little yawn.

"Will . . . it . . . soon . . . be . . . day . . . break?"

He put his tail over his head and before you could say "ninety-nine nuts", he was fast asleep.

DANIEL THE LION was a bit of a dreamer. His jungle friends teased him about it. "Here comes dreamy Daniel!" Ella Elephant said one sunny morning. "He always has his head in the clouds."

"I can't think what he has to dream about all day," Bertie Bear agreed. "We're all far too busy for daydreaming."

All the animals laughed at Daniel as he padded by, but he didn't mind. Sometimes it was fun to daydream.

He had a favourite dream when he went out on his early morning jog around the jungle. He would pretend he was running in the Olympics and, of course, he always came first and won a medal!

At noon when the sun was at its hottest, all the animals would crawl into the shade to escape the heat. It was so hot no-one could do a thing except lie there, panting.

That's where my daydreaming helps, Daniel thought to himself. He would imagine he was playing on an icy, snow-covered mountain. It always helped to keep him feeling cool.

One night, just as the baby animals were being put to bed, a big storm blew up.

The jungle leaves rustled and shook in the wind. The sky crackled with lightning and thunder roared.

"Don't worry. It's only a thunderstorm," Ella Elephant told her baby, Edwin, as she tucked him into bed. "Go to sleep now."

But little Edwin couldn't settle at all.

Meanwhile, under the tall trees, Milly Monkey and Bertie Bear were telling their youngsters the same thing.

"There's nothing to worry about," Bertie told his two baby bear cubs."

But it seemed that none of the little ones could sleep that night. Soon the jungle was filled with the sound of crying, as well as loud thunderclaps.

"Oh dear, what shall we do?" Ella Elephant sighed. "Our babies will be exhausted by morning."

To everyone's surprise, Daniel appeared and offered to help.

"You!" The animals gasped. "All you can do is daydream!"

"That's right," Daniel replied with a grin. "And I can fill your babies' heads with lovely sleepy dreams!"

Daniel went and sat beside little Edwin's bed.

"Close your eyes," he told him. "I have a lovely dream just for you. You're splashing in the river and squirting water all over your friends!"

Much to everyone's amazement, Edwin smiled and then fell asleep.

DANIEL, can you please help my bear cubs?" Bertie Bear asked.

Daniel nodded and sat on the bear cubs' bed.

"Here's the perfect dream for you two," he said. "It's a dream filled with pots of delicious, runny honey."

The little bear cubs licked their lips and moments later they were snoring soundly.

It didn't stop there. Daniel filled all the baby animals' heads with beautiful, exciting, sleepy dreams.

The tigers dreamt that they were brave explorers and the turtles . . . The dreams went on and on.

After that no-one ever teased Daniel about his daydreaming. And if you snuggle down in your nice warm bed, perhaps you can imagine what dreams Daniel might whisper in your ear.

If you listen very carefully, you too will soon be fast asleep!

SURPRISE!

"Have you decided what you would like for your birthday this year?" Gemma's mummy and daddy asked her one tea time.

Gemma took a big bite of her chocolate cake and thought hard. There wasn't really anything she wanted. She had plenty of toys and games. She'd been given the pair of silver roller-skates she'd longed for at Christmas and was still having lots of fun with them.

"I know," she said at last. "I'd love a big surprise."

"Are you sure?" Daddy asked.

"Yes," Gemma replied.

"Very well," Mummy said. "But promise me you won't go creeping around the house looking in all the cupboards. If you find your present, it won't be a proper surprise."

Gemma agreed, but as her birthday grew nearer, she couldn't help feeling curious, so she started to keep an eye open for clues!

One afternoon she arrived home from her friend's house to find Mummy with her sewing machine out. The minute she saw Gemma, she hurriedly hid what she was sewing.

"Making anything exciting?" Gemma asked.

"Nothing special," Mummy said.

Gemma knew her mummy was hiding something — maybe she was making something for Gemma's room.

The following day, Gemma's daddy seemed to be busy, too. He was in the shed and wouldn't even let Gemma bring him a mug of tea.

"What are you making?" Gemma called.

"Nothing special," he replied.

Gemma couldn't resist peeping through the window. He was sawing some wood.

"I bet it's a doll's house!" she decided.

But Gemma was even more confused when Gran and Grandad called round. They brought a mysterious-looking box. When nobody was looking she gave the box a little shake. It rattled like china! Could it be ornaments for her room?

"Guessed yet?" Mummy and Daddy chorused.

She shook her head. This present really was going to be a surprise!

The day before her birthday, Gemma's mummy took her out for the afternoon. They didn't arrive home again until it was quite dark outside. By now, Gemma was very excited. She still hadn't managed to find out what her present was!

At last it was morning.

"Happy birthday!" her mummy and daddy said when she came down to breakfast. "See if you can find your present!"

Gemma searched the house, but there was nothing in any of the rooms. Then, when she went out into the garden, she couldn't believe her eyes.

"A tree house!" she gasped.

She climbed up the rope ladder and looked inside.

It was a lovely little wooden house with pretty curtains at the door, tied back with ribbon.

Inside, there was a tiny wooden table with a china teaset all laid out.

"So that's why you've both been so busy!" She laughed. "I never guessed."

As she sat happily in her tree house, she decided that surprises really did make the best presents of all.

SOUTH of the Sahara in a hot dry land Gita, the giraffe, lived with her three best friends. There was Peter the porcupine, Anita the antelope and Zita the zebra.

One day Gita saw a lot of birds in the sky. They flew past in formation. She watched in admiration.

"It's a wonderful display!" Anita said.

"You don't see that

Gita Does The Loopy Loop

every day!" Zita agreed.

"They look as if they're dancing in the sky," Gita said. She thought for a minute.

"I know!" she said. "Let's give a dance display!"

Peter rattled his spines.

"I'm not going to dance in the sky!" he said.

"I'm sorry but neither am I," Anita said.

"What nonsense!" Zita said. "You know we can't fly!"

"We'll dance on the ground, of course," Gita said. "We'll start straight away!"

"But it's time for my quill cleaning," Peter declared.

"It's time for grass nibbling," Anita said.

"It's time for my morning run," Zita said.

"Oh, come on!" Gita said. "It'll be fun."

She kicked her long legs and did a lively jive.

It did look fun. Soon everyone began to dance.

PETER showed them how to do the Rumba and the Conga, and then the Hokey-Cokey.

"This is okey-dokey!" he cried.

He shook his spines and did the Quill-Quiver. He made such a breeze that he blew all the leaves out of the trees.

They covered him completely, you could only see his nose. It took ages to uncover him, but at last they saw his toes.

"Let's start again!" Gita said.

Anita did the Foxtrot and the Quickstep, and a stately Minuet.

"And I haven't finished yet," she said.

She danced about and did the Two-Horn-Twist, but her horns got caught in the tree. It took ages to unhook her but they did it before tea.

"We'll have to start again," said Gita.

Zita did the Tango and the Polka, and a rather slow Mazurka.

"I'm a slow and steady worker," she explained.

She tapped her feet and did the Stripey-Shuffle.

In fact she caused a bit of a kerfuffle, because she shuffled up a sandstorm and disappeared from sight. It took ages to locate her — well into the night.

I'll show you how to dance," Gita said.

She did the Stomp and Jitterbug, and a bit of Rock-and-Roll. She coiled her neck and did the Loopy Loop.

AND then she really felt silly because she twisted such a lot, she tied herself in a big knot.

It took ages to undo it.

"We'll never get this right," she said, with a sigh.

Suddenly, Leo, the lion, appeared.

Everybody jumped.

"I'm an expert at the Nocturnal Prowl," he growled. "I do it every night when I'm looking for my supper." He licked his lips. "I'll show you how it's done."

"Th—thanks," Gita stuttered. "M—make room everyone!"

They moved back . . . and back . . . and back . . . and then they ran as fast as they could, until Leo was out of sight.

"That gave me quite a fright!" Gita said.

She ate some leaves to calm her nerves and Anita nibbled grass. Peter cleaned his quills and Zita got ready for a run.

"That's enough dancing for me!" Gita said. And her friends all agreed!

91

Ellie's Treasure

WHEN Ellie lost the little bird brooch that her auntie had given her for her birthday she was very upset.

It had been pinned on to the collar of her favourite jacket, but when Mummy took the jacket down from its hook in the hall cupboard, the brooch wasn't there.

Although they searched everywhere, they couldn't find it.

"Never mind," Mummy said. "We'll buy another one."

"But it won't be the same," Ellie said. "That one was my treasure. It came all the way from Canada and Auntie Jenny said that it flew across the ocean."

Later, when they were getting ready to go to the park, Ellie looked out of the window and saw a rainbow.

"There's treasure at the end of the rainbow, isn't there?" she asked Mummy.

"How do you know that?"

"Because I heard a story about it. Do you think my bird brooch is at the end of the rainbow?" she asked.

"It may be," Mummy said. "But the end of the rainbow is very hard to find."

"No, it isn't. It's only just behind those houses across the road," Ellie said. "Can we go and look, Mummy? Please can we go to look for my bird brooch?"

"All right," Mummy agreed. "We'll go to look, but the end of the rainbow is never where you think it is."

MUMMY and Ellie put on their coats and walked together up the road. But, as they tried to get closer to the rainbow, it seemed to move away from them.

"It isn't behind those houses now. It's gone up on to the top of the hill," Ellie said. "I think it wants us to chase it. Shall we run after it?"

"We could try," Mummy said.

So, Mummy and Ellie ran up the hill towards the park, but soon they had to stop because Mummy was out of breath.

But the rainbow seemed to be waiting for them at the top of the hill.

"Come on!" Ellie called, tugging at Mummy's hand. "Don't let it get away."

They hurried up the hill to the very top, but when they got there they saw that the rainbow had run down the other side and it was shining very brightly on the park.

"There it is," Ellie exclaimed. "There's the end of the rainbow, just by the swings."

She ran down the hill ahead of Mummy, keeping her eye on the place where the rainbow seemed to touch the ground.

She was sure that she would find her bird brooch there. When they reached the park, Ellie ran towards the place in the playground where she was sure she would find her treasure.

SHE knelt down, searching the ground all around for her bird brooch. Then, suddenly, the sun became brighter and the rain stopped.

When she looked up, the rainbow was fading away and in a moment it had completely disappeared.

"Oh, no," she declared. "I'll never find my bird brooch now that the rainbow's gone."

Ellie and Mummy walked home. Ellie was very sad and Mummy promised she could have some ice-cream after her tea to cheer her up.

As they reached home it began to rain again.

"Hang up your coat in the hall cupboard," Mummy said.

As Ellie crossed the hall the sun shone through the window and on to a crystal vase Mummy kept on the windowsill. Ellie saw a lovely rainbow appear on the floor.

"Look!" she called to her mummy. "The rainbow's come into the house!"

As she knelt down to look at the colours, she saw something glint on the carpet.

"Mummy!" she called. "I've found it! I've found my bird brooch and it really was at the end of the rainbow."

93

Teeth For Charlie Frog

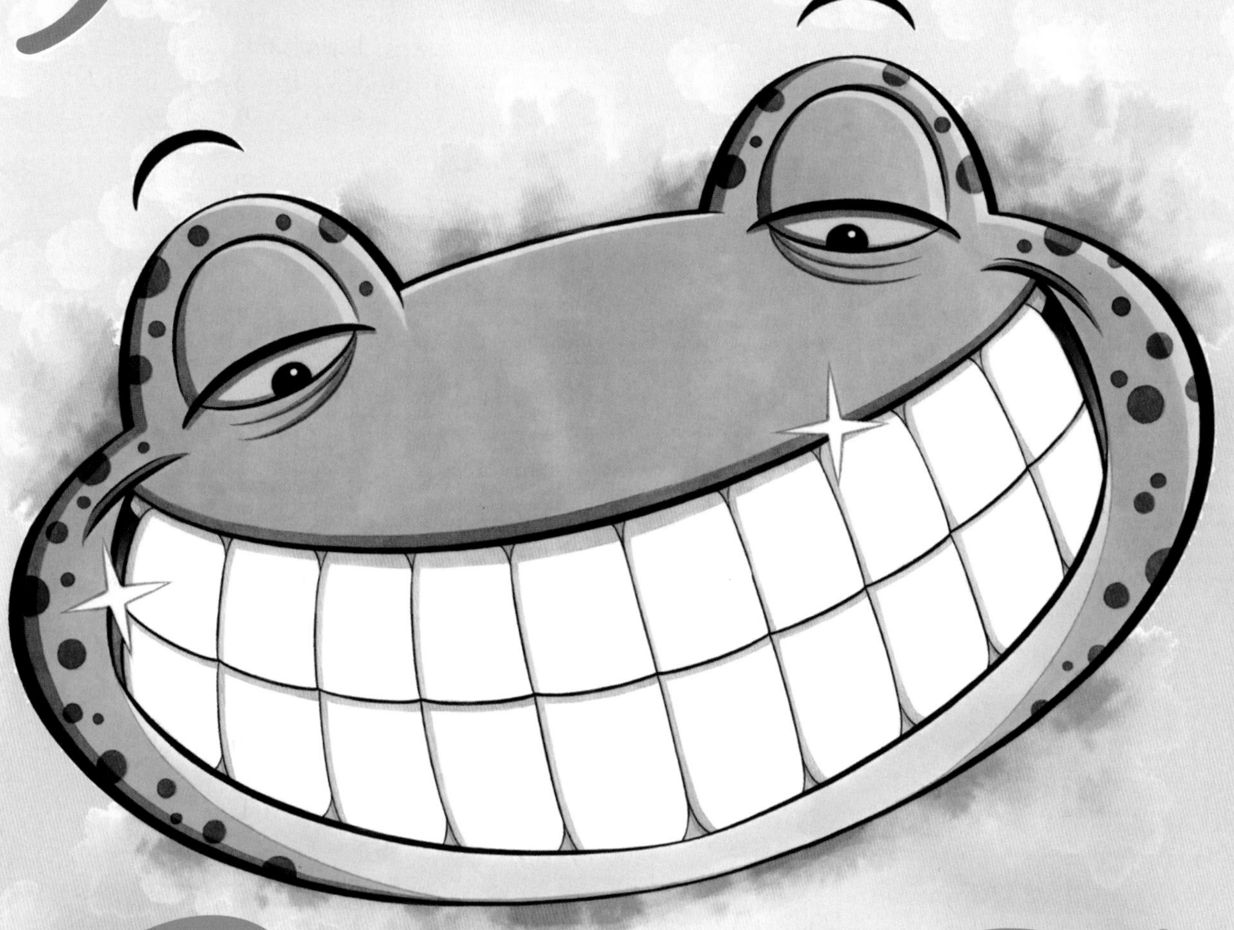

CHARLIE FROG hopped sadly along the grassy bank of the stream. He saw Sam Squirrel sitting near a tree. Sam was holding a nut between his two front paws.

"Hello, Charlie. Why are you so sad?"

"I want teeth, Sam," Charlie said, looking up at the pretty grey squirrel.

"Why?"

"Everyone has teeth."

"Charlie, frogs don't need teeth to eat insects," Sam Squirrel said, "but I need teeth to chew these nuts."

A kingfisher was perched on the branch above.

"I don't need teeth," he cried. He dived into the water and flew off with a small fish in his beak.

"I told you, Charlie," Sam said. "Lots of creatures don't have teeth."

A fox trotted down to the water's edge. He lapped up some water.

"That's good," he said, licking his lips.

"I do wish I had teeth like yours, Mister Fox," Charlie said longingly.

The fox's sharp white teeth gleamed and his thick red tail wagged slowly.

"Try the Tooth Fairy," he said with a wide smile. "She buys teeth from little boys and girls when they don't need them any more."

"I know where she lives," Sam Squirrel said. "Come on, Charlie."

"Thank you, Mister Fox," Charlie said as he hopped away.

An hour later they reached the Tooth Fairy's home.

"Tooth Fairy," Charlie called. "Could I please talk to you?"

Out flew a tiny fairy. She folded her wings together like a butterfly and landed in front of them.

"Can I help you?" she asked.

"Isn't she pretty?" Sam whispered.

"I want to have teeth," Charlie told her. "Will you help me, please?"

"Frogs don't need teeth, Charlie," she replied.

Charlie was surprised. How did the Tooth Fairy know his name?

"Fairies know everything," Sam whispered.

"I would like to be able to bite and chew food," Charlie went on.

"I don't like this one little bit," the Tooth Fairy said, looking worried.

She waved her wand over Charlie's head. Suddenly Charlie had teeth! He was so excited.

"Thank you, Tooth Fairy. You have made me so happy," Charlie said. "We will go home now."

"Speak up, Charlie," Sam said, puzzled. "You are mumbling."

"It's these teeth," Charlie said slowly and carefully. "I'm not used to them yet."

"Let's go home, Charlie," Sam Squirrel said. "I'm hungry."

"So am I." Charlie's long tongue flicked out for a fly.

"Ouch!" he cried. The fly flew out of his mouth. "I bit my tongue!"

"I can't close my mouth," he told Sam. "My jaws ache, and my tongue is sore."

"That's because you don't have the right kind of mouth for teeth," Sam said sternly.

CHARLIE grabbed another fly. "Ouch!" he cried as he bit his tongue again. "I'm so hungry."

"Try a nut," Sam said.

"It doesn't taste nice." Charlie threw it away.

"You will have to learn to like chewy things," Sam told him. "You can't catch insects with those big teeth."

Charlie tasted some berries, and threw them away.

"I don't like them either."

"You can eat grass," Sam said cheerfully, "or corn or hay or wheat. That's what cows and horses eat."

"Never," Charlie said. He sat down and cried. "I don't want these teeth!"

"Hello, Charlie," the Tooth Fairy said softly, hovering just above his head. "Why are you crying?"

"I can't catch insects," Charlie moaned. "I'm so hungry. My jaws ache. My tongue is sore."

He looked up at the Tooth Fairy hopefully.

The Tooth Fairy waved her wand and the teeth were gone. Charlie closed his mouth.

"Have you learned your lesson now?" the Tooth Fairy demanded.

"Oh, yes," Charlie said happily. "Frogs don't need teeth. I am happy just as I am."

95

Georgia's Garden

IT was a bright sunny morning when Georgia woke up.

After breakfast Daddy said he was going to do some gardening.

"Why don't you come out and help me?" he asked Georgia. "I could do with some help — the garden's a jungle!"

Georgia found her green wellies and followed Daddy down the garden path. The garden was in a mess! It hadn't been touched for months.

"Where shall I start?" Georgia asked.

"You could pull up that row of dead flowers and weeds," Daddy decided.

Georgia set to work and, to her delight, a little robin flew down to join her.

"Look, Daddy," she said. "There's a robin right beside my feet. He isn't a bit afraid of me."

"He'll be looking out for grubs and insects you've pulled up with the weeds," Daddy said. "Robins are the gardener's friend!"

Next, Georgia decided to tidy up the rockery. She had another surprise.

"Oh!" She squealed as a tiny frog hopped out. Then she discovered another in a rain-filled flower pot.

"Come over here, Daddy!" she called.

"How funny!" Daddy said. "It's found its own pond in a plant pot!"

She decided to leave the pots where they were as she liked the idea of frogs living in her garden.

It was hard work doing the gardening. Then, all of a sudden, Georgia saw something move when she tugged away a chunk of ivy.

"Daddy, quick!" she called. "Come and see before it slithers away."

Daddy came running. He just caught a glimpse of the grass snake before it slipped under the fence.

"Well done for spotting that!" Daddy said to Georgia. "Grass snakes are hard to find. He's quite harmless and really very shy."

Georgia had thought she didn't like snakes, but that one was so small and such a pretty colour she couldn't dislike it.

"I didn't know gardening could be so exciting!" she said to Daddy.

GEORGIA went to look for a rake as there were lots of leaves on the lawn to sweep up.

As she was sweeping, she felt the rake catch something. It was an old bird's nest.

"It must have blown down during the winter," Daddy said.

GEORGIA had never seen a bird's nest close up before. She was surprised how neatly the strands of grass and twigs had been woven together. She picked up the nest and wedged it back in the apple tree.

"Perhaps another bird can come along and use it," she said.

"We could build a nesting box for the tree," Daddy suggested. "It wouldn't take long to make. There's lots of spare wood in the shed."

Later that afternoon Georgia and Daddy looked around their garden. It was much tidier and there was a brand new nesting box in the apple tree.

"You are right about the garden being a jungle," Georgia laughed. "It's full of wildlife!"

"And surprises!" Daddy said. "Look, I found the first strawberries at the back of the fence. There's one for Mummy, one for me and two for you!"

Happily Georgia skipped inside to share her good news with Mummy.

97

If A Giant Came To Tea

98

"LET'S pretend," Mum said to me,
  "To ask a giant home to tea!
  "He couldn't stand – he'd be too tall,
"His feet would reach into the hall.

"He'd eat so much, at such a rate,
"What would we give him for a plate?
"What would he use to eat his food?
"To use his fingers would be rude!

"Our knives and forks would be too small,
"They'd be no use to him at all.
"Just think – where a knife and fork were laid,
"Instead we'd have to put a garden spade!

"No cup would do, from which to drink,
"He'd have to use our kitchen sink!
"The giant would eat such loads of tea,
"There'd be none left," I said, "for me!"
"Not one bit left in all the house
"To feed even the smallest mouse!"

It wouldn't work, you must agree,
To ask a giant home to tea.
So mum says she'll just go and phone
And tell him, "We are not at home!"

ACTIVITY

What do you think the face of a giant would be like? Use this space to draw your ideas. Remember, all his features would be bigger than yours!

IT was summer and tiny fluffy white clouds drifted along in the otherwise clear blue sky.

But Natalie, the Christmas fairy, couldn't see the sky. She'd been in the back of Gemma's toy cupboard in the middle of some sparkling gold and silver tinsel and other pretty decorations since last Christmas.

"I wish I could be a summer fairy instead of a Christmas fairy." Natalie sighed. "Then I wouldn't have to wait until Christmas to come out of this cupboard. I could sit on top of the Christmas tree now!

"Also, if I was a summer fairy, the sun could shine on the star at the top of my wand and make it glow." Natalie smiled at that lovely thought.

It wasn't long before Natalie's wish was granted. The very next day, Gemma decided to tidy her toy cupboard and began taking everything out of it.

Gemma didn't notice Natalie in the middle of the Christmas decorations when she took them downstairs and put them on top of a table ready to sort out.

Natalie couldn't believe her luck. At last her wish had come true! She could now really be a summer fairy!

She blinked as she gazed at the sun streaming in through the window.

Then she looked all around her for the Christmas tree, but somehow it had disappeared! There were no decorations around the room either, so it didn't look nearly as pretty as it did each Christmas. Natalie felt quite disappointed.

Because Natalie had never been out of the cupboard in the summer before, she had no idea how hot the sun could be.

Soon she felt so hot that tiny droplets of water trickled down her forehead. Then she got hotter and hotter until she thought she might melt!

WHAT a shock she had, though, when the sun shone upon the star at the top of her wand. It glowed so much that she could see her face in it. And her face was glowing bright red!

Suddenly, Natalie didn't want to be a summer fairy. Summer was much too hot. Besides, without a Christmas tree she wouldn't be able to enjoy spending hours on top of it, gazing down at all the pretty different coloured balls on its branches.

Now, more than anything else, Natalie wanted to be back inside the nice cool toy cupboard again.

It wasn't long before Gemma picked up all the Christmas decorations ready to put them back neatly inside the toy cupboard once more. It was then that she noticed Natalie.

"You shouldn't be out here yet," Gemma told her. "It's much too soon. It's still summer and Christmas is months away."

Then, to Natalie's delight, Gemma gently placed her at the back of the toy cupboard. Natalie was happy to be back among the sparkling gold and silver tinsel and the other pretty Christmas decorations once more.

In fact, ever since that day, she's been so happy being a Christmas fairy that she only ever wants to come out of the toy cupboard at Christmas!

Woo's
Words
Of
Wisdom

WOO, the wise old owl, had just arrived back at his favourite tree after a night spent hunting when he noticed his friend, Mrs Bunny Rabbit. She was standing by the entrance of her burrow, frowning.

"What's the matter, Mrs Bunny?" he asked. "You do look worried."

"Yes, I am worried, Woo," she replied. "I can't stop the draught whistling down the passageway into my little home. We are all feeling cold."

"Couldn't you move to a warmer burrow?" Woo suggested. "There must be some empty ones which are not so draughty."

Mrs Bunny shook her head.

"No, they are all taken. We'll just have to make do with this one and try to stop the draughts somehow. But I have nothing suitable for stopping draughts."

Woo thought for a moment.

"What about putting some straw in the entrance? That might work."

Mrs Bunny said she had tried that, but the draught just blew the straw into her living-room and she had to keep clearing up the mess!

Woo was feeling sleepy, so he said he would try to think of something and come back later to see her. Mrs Bunny invited him to come to tea at four o'clock so that he could see for himself how bad the problem was. Woo was happy to accept.

Just before he went to sleep, Woo thought more about Mrs Bunny's problem. He remembered something his wise old grandmother used to say. She always said there was a solution to everything. Woo also thought of another saying of hers.

"If you haven't got a lot, make the best of what you've got!"

Promptly at four o'clock Woo called at Mrs Bunny's house. He felt the draught as soon as he entered the burrow. It blew right down the passageway into the living-room. The living-room looked very cosy, but the draught seemed to blow away any heat that the fire produced!

A table was set for tea and Mrs Bunny had made some seed cakes and a big pot of tea. It looked very inviting.

"Have you thought of anything?" Mrs Bunny asked when they had finished their tea.

"Well, I did remember something my old grandmother used to say," Woo replied. "She said we should use what we have and make the best of it."

"But I haven't got anything to use, Woo," Mrs Bunny said. "You can see how little there is here. My little ones need an extra bedcover each to keep them warm and I need curtains for the window. What could I use?"

Woo looked around him. He saw a box of tiny bits of material — the pieces all too small to be of any use on their own.

"I know what we can do," he suggested. "We'll sew these pieces of cloth together and make patchwork bedcovers and curtains. We can make a strong curtain to hang up by your front door to keep the draught out."

Mrs Bunny was surprised to learn that she actually had something which could be used to make the house cosier. She got her needles and threads out right away and started joining the little pieces of cloth together as Woo had suggested.

Woo helped, too, and very soon they had made bedcovers for the children's beds. Then they got started on the big curtain for the front door.

By evening time it was ready. Woo fixed it up on hooks for Mrs Bunny and it worked perfectly. It stopped the wind howling down the passageway and Mrs Bunny's home became much warmer.

MRS BUNNY was so pleased that her problem had been solved that she decided to make a surprise present for Woo with the rest of the cloth. Woo was delighted with the present — a lovely cushion which made his favourite perch more comfortable.

And Woo was very glad that he had been able to help his friend, all thanks to his dear old grandmother's words of wisdom.

103

The Clockmaker

D ANIEL had learned to tell the time with the help of the old cuckoo clock that hung on the wall. The clock looked like a little wooden house, but the windows were just painted on.

The tiny door was real, though. Every hour it flew open and the brightly-painted wooden cuckoo came out to tell the time.

"Cuckoo! Cuckoo! Cuckoo!"

And Daniel would shout, "Three o'clock!"

Daniel had learned that the big hand of the clock always pointed to the top when it was time for the cuckoo to come out. When the big hand was getting close, Daniel would stand and wait for the door to open.

"Cuckoo! Cuckoo! Cuckoo! Cuckoo!"

Daniel would shout, "Four o'clock!"

But one day, when the big hand reached the top, nothing happened! Daniel stared at the little door but it did not open. The cuckoo did not come out. He ran to tell his mum what had happened.

"I think our clock might need mending," his mum said. "We will take it to the clockmaker this afternoon."

After lunch Daniel helped his mum pack the cuckoo clock into a big shopping basket and they set off for town.

DANIEL had never been to a clockmaker's shop before. There were all sorts of clocks everywhere. Big clocks, tall clocks, shiny clocks, glass clocks where he could see the works going round inside, and even one or two cuckoo clocks.

The clockmaker smiled at Daniel and his mum.

"How can I help?" he asked.

Mum took the cuckoo clock from the basket and the clockmaker placed it down on his bench. Very carefully he took off the back of the clock and peered inside.

"Ah, yes, I think I can see the problem," he said. "I should be able to fix this for you right away."

Daniel watched as the clockmaker poked at something inside the clock with a long thin screwdriver. Then he replaced the back on the clock and pushed the big hand up to the top. The little door flew open and the cuckoo shot out.

"Cuckoo! Cuckoo! Cuckoo! Cuckoo! Cuckoo!"

"Five o'clock!" Daniel shouted.

The clockmaker laughed.

"Do you like cuckoo clocks?" the friendly clockmaker asked Daniel.

Daniel nodded.

"Yes, but I didn't know there were so many other kinds of clocks!"

"They all have their own voices, too," the clockmaker told him.

He pointed to a tall grandfather clock in the corner. It was taller than Mum. It was even taller than the clockmaker. It was much, much taller than Daniel.

"What do you suppose he sounds like?" the clockmaker asked.

Daniel shook his head.

"I don't know."

The clockmaker walked over to the grandfather clock and moved the big hand up to the top.

"BONG! BONG! BONG!" went the clock, so loudly that it made Daniel and his mum jump.

Daniel had still managed to count, though, and he shouted, "Three o'clock!"

"Quite right," the clockmaker said. "How about this one?"

HE pointed to a tiny golden clock on the counter and pushed its thin big hand to the top.

"Ting! Ting! Ting!" went the little clock so quietly that Daniel had to listen really carefully to count.

"Three o'clock again!" he shouted.

"You certainly know about clocks!" The clockmaker smiled. "Perhaps you will grow up to be a clockmaker."

Daniel had not considered that, but as he carried his cuckoo clock back home he thought about it a lot. And now, when anyone asks him what he wants to be when he grows up, he knows just what to say.

105

Freddie's

FREDDIE FROG was sitting on the edge of his pond with his friend Philip. They were eating their lunch of pond weed and pond water.

Usually Freddie liked his pond food, but today he thought the food tasted dull.

Adventure

"I'm tired of this old stuff," he said to Philip. "I want something different for a change. I wonder what sea water tastes like?"

"I think it's a bit salty," Philip said. " And Sammy Seagull said that seaweed is really tough and tastes just horrid."

"Well I'd like to try it," Freddie said. "Will you come with me to the seaside?"

Philip shook his head and said he'd much rather stay where he was. He had no wish to taste the sea.

BUT Freddie was determined to go. He said goodbye to Philip and began the long hop to the seaside.

First of all he had to hop across the field where Farmer Smith kept his bull. Freddie nearly turned back when the bull started to roar, but he was so keen to get to the seaside that he hopped bravely on.

Then he came to a busy street and the noise was terrible. He watched all the children crossing when the green man was showing and he hopped safely over the road with them.

Then he came to the beach which was covered in stones with sandy patches in between.

The stones hurt his webbed feet when he hopped on them and when he jumped on to the sand he was nearly buried. But he went bravely on and suddenly there was the sea.

Freddie couldn't believe how big it was. It was the biggest thing he had ever seen. Now that he had reached the sea, he was determined to taste the water.

He settled down by the edge of the water and took a bite of some brown seaweed he found there.

"Cro-o-o-ak! It's horrid. I must have a drink to get rid of the taste!"

He bent down and took a long sip of sea water.

"Yuk!" he yelled. "It's terrible. He watched all the horrid. I wish I'd never come here."

Poor Freddie! He was so disappointed.

"I'm going back home," he said. "My pond is far nicer."

HE hopped back over the sand and stones, he hopped across the noisy road when the green man was showing and he hopped over the farmer's field where the bull was grazing.

He was so keen to get home that he didn't notice what a long way it was.

At last he took one last big hop and landed on the edge of his own little pond, right next to Philip.

"Welcome home Freddie," Philip said. "Would you like some supper? We'll have pond weed and pond water."

"Yes, please," Freddie said. "That would be lovely."

And it was — and Freddie never wanted to go away from his little pond, ever again.

107

The Red Umbrella

KATIE had bought a red umbrella with her birthday money. She was very proud of it. She showed Stephen how she pushed the little catch with her fingers and it shot up into the air. Whoosh!

All around the edge of the umbrella were children chasing each other playing catch. They were laughing and having fun.

The artist had painted brightly coloured dresses for the girls with matching hair ribbons and slides. The boys were wearing shorts and jeans and t-shirts.

Stephen wished he had a red umbrella like Katie's. His birthday wasn't for ages. He thought that by then there wouldn't be any umbrellas like this left in the shop.

Mum had given him her old grey one but it just wasn't the same. He thought perhaps he could paint a picture on it himself but Mum said no, that wouldn't work, because as soon as it rained all the colours would run off.

Katie couldn't wait for a wet day. She would stand in the garden wearing the pretty blue shoes Gran had given her, twirling her new umbrella round and round and round, and all the children would run faster and faster in their game of catch.

"Watch me!" she called out to her brother. "Come on. Come and see what I'm doing. I'm making all the children come out to play!"

"Go on," Mum said to Stephen. "Maybe Katie will give you a turn. You could let her play with your train."

But Katie didn't want to. She couldn't help it. She just liked her new umbrella too much. She went on twirling it high in the air.

"I can't wait for it to rain!" she said.

And it did rain, the very next Saturday.

Mum always took the children to town on Saturday afternoons while Dad went to watch a football match. He was going to take Stephen with him one day but Stephen was too small to see anything over the heads in the crowd so Dad said it would be better to wait a bit longer.

Stephen was really looking forward to that. He liked going to town with Mum, though. She said he could wear his yellow wellies but Katie wanted to wear her pretty blue shoes.

TODAY, as usual, after all the shopping was done they went to a café and had ice-cream, strawberry for Katie and chocolate for Stephen.

Mum always had a cup of tea. When they came out of the café it was raining really heavily. Katie gave a great whoop of joy and pressed the little catch to make the red umbrella shoot up.

All the wet people passing by smiled at them as Katie spun round and round, calling, "Look at me! Look at me! See, I'm dancing with all the boys and girls!"

THEN, quite suddenly, a big gust of wind caught the red umbrella and with a whoosh it rose out of Katie's hand and bowled along the pavement. The children ran after it and found it sitting right in the middle of a puddle.

A really big puddle.

Katie started to cry because she was going to spoil her pretty blue shoes if she tried to rescue it.

Her kind brother put his arm round her shoulders and then jumped into the puddle. The water came nearly to the top of his wellies but he didn't mind. He grabbed the umbrella and shook it, then brought it safely back to Katie who was smiling again.

"Oh, thank you, thank you," she cried. "Now it's your turn, Stephen!"

Then she clapped her hands as Stephen twirled and twirled the red umbrella and all the painted girls and boys raced round in their game of catch as they came out to play especially for him!